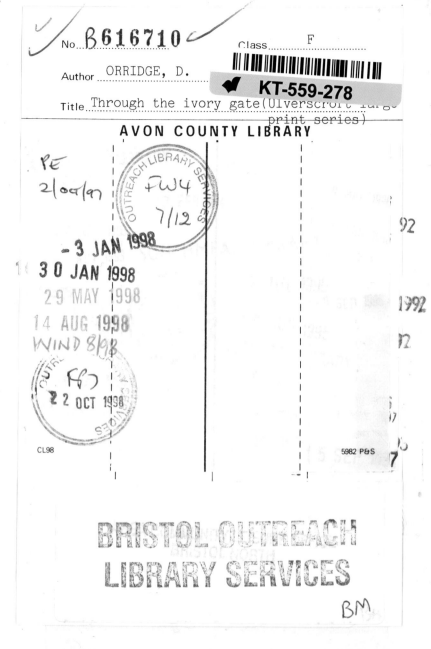

Love is
a time of enchantment:
in it all days are fair and all fields
green. Youth is blest by it,
old age made benign: the eyes of love see
roses blooming in December,
and sunshine through rain. Verily
is the time of true-love
a time of enchantment—and
Oh! how eager is woman
to be bewitched!

THROUGH THE IVORY GATE

Rachel Verity finds life in the mining village far from dull. At times it is as stark and ugly as the colliery winding gear which dominates the scene. But there is beauty in the surrounding countryside, beauty which is directly responsible for the jealousy and treachery which Rachel encounters. Fortunately she has her friends, David, gentle and effeminate, Rupert, a bird-watcher, and the irrepressible Luke who works "regular nightshifts" at the pit. But it is Marilyn who changes Rachel's life, for her gibe about her having no sex-appeal is a challenge.

DIA ORRIDGE

THROUGH THE IVORY GATE

Complete and Unabridged

ULVERSCROFT
Leicester

First published in Great Britain in 1975 by
Robert Hale Ltd.,
London

First Large Print Edition
published September 1989

British Library CIP Data

Orridge, Dia
    Through the ivory gate—Large print ed.—
    Ulverscroft large print series: romance
    I. Title
    823'.914[F]

    ISBN 0-7089-2062-4

Published by
F. A. Thorpe (Publishing) Ltd.
Anstey, Leicestershire
Set by Rowland Phototypesetting Ltd.
Bury St. Edmunds, Suffolk
Printed and bound in Great Britain by
T. J. Press (Padstow) Ltd., Padstow, Cornwall

Dreams out of the ivory gate
and visions before midnight.
SIR THOMAS BROWNE

1

RACHEL VERITY looked at the man who had just come in, and a strange, shivering excitement swept over her.

She watched as he waved away the smoked salmon sandwiches, the prawn *vol-au-vents*, smilingly accepted a drink, and joked with the women fluttering around him.

Was it her imagination or had the atmosphere lightened? Were people really smiling more?

Rachel poked at the slice of lemon in her drink and absent-mindedly sucked her finger tip. It was a childish gesture oddly at variance with the simple sophistication of her sea-green frock and crisply cut black hair.

She watched Lena Sefton move in, kiss the man and cling possessively to his free arm.

Darting a glance at Henry Sefton, Lena's husband, who a moment before had been rocking perilously back on his heels, glass in hand, a blob of spittle on his lower lip as he held forth about blood-sports and the foxes which had killed twenty of his chickens, Rachel noticed he had stopped rocking. There was a fixed, glassy look in his eyes.

"Poison the blighters. It's the only way," he muttered.

Rachel stared at him a startled moment longer then her eyebrows shot up as the stranger shook himself free of Lena, moved forward and kissed Amy Forrester, Rachel's aunt, who was standing a little apart from the rest.

Aunt Amy! Cool, assured, but *freckled* and at least thirty-five!

The man was near enough now for her to see the contrast between the deeply tanned skin, the small, dark eyes, bright and alert like a thrush's, and the shock of silver hair. His nose was big and bony, his hands soft, his manner gentle.

Again Rachel felt a shiver run through her, as though some chemical reaction over which she had no control had started deep within her. Vaguely, she heard Henry Sefton muttering to himself; was aware of conversation going on around her; of glasses being filled.

A few moments later Amy moved away. The stranger stood alone, looking around him.

Rachel willed him to look in her direction.

She saw his gaze rest fractionally on Mary Hornsby, quiet, practical Mary, picking up the threads of her life again after her recent widowhood. He looked for much longer on Marilyn, a girl as delectable as her namesake, then his gaze slid round the room and came to rest on Rachel.

At first she looked coolly back at him but there was something so calculating and impersonal in his expression she became embarrassed. As he continued to stare, her embarrassment turned to resentment. She tried to look haughty but the unexpected turmoil within her made it difficult.

Resisting an almost compelling desire to go to him, she smiled faintly, and to make her indifference quite clear, lifted her glass to her lips and tilted back her head.

Unfortunately, apart from the slice of

lemon which slid down and hit her on the nose, her glass was empty.

Flustered, she turned her back. Now! Any moment he would be by her side offering his hanky, offering to get her another drink. She waited. The lemon juice was making her nose tickle. She gave it a quick rub with the back of her hand.

When he didn't materialise she frowned, sauntered over to a small table, put down her glass and turned, ready to shrivel him with a glance.

It was a moment or two before she saw him on the far side of the room, one arm across Marilyn's shoulders, the other holding a fully charged glass.

"Well! the slithy tove!"

A woman's laugh exploded near by, startling her. "I see J.B.'s made another conquest."

The voice was loud, metallic. Lena Sefton stepped from the shadow of an alcove, her tawny eyes alight with malicious amusement.

Rachel gave her a swift appraising glance and knew that war had been declared.

4

"I don't know what you are talking about," she said.

"Oh come come, my dear. It was a good try, but you were rather obvious. And with J.B. of all people." Lena put a hand under her thick mane of hair and flicked it off her shoulders. The movement was full of confidence.

"J.B.?"

"Jonathan Blake, the artist. Don't tell me you didn't know?"

Rachel's mouth shaped an "O" but she made no sound. So that's who he is? She nodded slowly, confirming her own thoughts. Jonathan Blake. Amy had mentioned him casually over a cup of chocolate during Rachel's first evening here in Lynbury.

"Our resident artist is away in Rome," she had said. And that was all. When Rachel had questioned her about him later, Amy had admitted that some of his paintings had been accepted by the Academy. He was now working on a portrait which he thought was the best work he had ever done. His subject was Lena Sefton.

I can't imagine why, thought Rachel.

5

She isn't beautiful. She isn't even pretty. Her nose is too long. Her eyelashes are straight, thick, but straight and she must be nearly as old as Amy.

Yet she had to admit the over-all impression was one of magnificence. Lena was alive with vanity and self-confidence. The tawny eyes a few shades lighter than the hair—the sinuous movements, the glowing skin. Dressed in a David Ramsey gown of bronze and black she reminded Rachel of Blake's poem (another Blake!) *"Tyger, Tyger, Burning Bright—"*

Lena's head was tilted back, her lips unsmiling yet parted to show her teeth, her expression insolent to the point of viciousness.

"Look your fill. I've got what it takes." Her voice was soft but Rachel felt a shock at having her thoughts read so easily. She smiled, determined to be friendly.

"Amy—Amy Forrester, my aunt, says J.B. is painting your portrait and it might be hung in the Academy. It must be terribly thrilling."

"Oh *terribly* thrilling." Lena's metallic drawl was heavy with sarcasm. "No doubt you are wondering what your chances are

6

of becoming his next model? Already you see yourself inspiring a major work which will bring fame and fortune to you both?" She laughed softly.

Rachel's cheeks flamed. Such a dream, fleeting and enjoyable, had flashed through her mind and she resented this girl's uncanny knack of reading her thoughts.

Yet despite Lena, she felt an extraordinary thrill when she remembered the way the artist had looked at her. A thrill which was followed quickly by the fear that she had offended him when she had turned her back.

Lena's eyes were mocking her, reading her innermost thoughts, waiting to tear to shreds her beautiful daydreams.

Refusing to be intimidated yet not wishing to quarrel, Rachel said the first thing which came into her head.

"Your husband's looking for you." She indicated with a nod of her head where Henry stood alone and disconsolate, twirling an empty glass.

Lena opened her eyes wide and treated her to a stare of concentrated fury. Rachel, trying hard to make her own brown eyes as compelling as Lena's, needed all her self-control not to look away.

In the end it was Lena who looked away. When next she spoke her voice had a playfulness not matched by her expression.

"Baby face," she said. "Stick to your own age group my dear. J.B. is not for you. Catch a fish you can fry."

Immediately Rachel recognised the phrase from a film she had seen on TV, the tension inside her snapped. She laughed.

Lena stared angrily. "What's so funny—?"

Rachel, with memories of dormitory squabbles fresh in her mind, looked at the older girl in amazement. "I'm surprised you find it necessary to talk to me like that. I can't help wondering if you have found your frying pan too small to hold him?"

"How *dare* you!" The words came out in an explosion of fury.

Rachel shrugged and walked away. There was an uncomfortable feeling between her shoulder blades where she imagined Lena's baleful glance was directed, and a feeling of shame in her heart because she had allowed herself a cheap victory.

For the rest of the evening she avoided Lena and the artist. This wasn't difficult for the party was being held in David Ramsey's spacious salon which had been created by knocking down the dividing wall between the dining-and drawing-rooms of this big Victorian house.

She looked at the white-painted walls, the gilt-framed mirrors, the crystal chand-eliers and the few pieces of white leather furniture with amber cushions whose colour was reflected in the masses of leaves standing in white vases in the alcoves.

It was a splendid background for the jewel-coloured frocks worn by the women and girls—most of them local—who had taken part in the dress show prior to the party.

Rachel smiled and waved at David as he came back into the room after seeing off Mr. Galbraith, the Yorkshire business man from whom he was hoping to win financial backing in order to start a small mass-production unit for his designs.

For despite his lilac suit and silk shirt,

his floppy fair hair and the exaggerated, mock-feminine voice he occasionally used to make people laugh (or to annoy them, depending on his mood and to whom he was talking) David was a tough young man who knew exactly where he was going.

Seeing Rachel's smile, he started to cross the room towards her but Lena intercepted him and seemed to be grumbling about her frock. Something to do with the fastening apparently.

Rachel watched with interest. She had helped with the finishing of that frock and there had been nothing wrong with it when it had been delivered to Lena.

Over Lena's shoulder, David gave her a reassuring wink. She winked back then turned and smiled politely at Mrs. Kaye, an elegant silvery blonde in a cerise trouser suit who had drifted up and was talking about her son, Rupert.

When *wasn't* she talking about him, thought Rachel crossly.

"I had another letter from him today," Mrs. Kaye was saying. "I told him you'd come to stay with Amy. He asked me to give you his love." She smiled at Rachel's look of surprise. "Not that he could possibly remember you. You were both such tiny tots when you were here last. I don't suppose you remember him do you?"

Not for the life of her could Rachel remember coming to Lynbury when she was a tiny tot. As for meeting a fellow tot named Rupert—But guessing what was expected of her she smiled. "Why, yes, I do remember a rather jolly little boy—"

Mrs. Kaye pounced. "That's right. That would be Rupert. He was full of fun. Still is. Fancy you remembering." She looked fondly at Rachel and began rummaging in her bag. "I have a snapshot of him some-where—unless it's in my other bag. Never mind, he'll be home next week. He'll be lecturing at the college you know—ornithology." She shut her bag with a loud snap.

Rachel stifled a groan. Ornithology! A bird-watcher named Rupert! How utterly brillig!

David joined them before she could comment. "Darling!" he said in his mock-feminine voice. "You *do* look cross. Stand up *straight* ducky. I've been watching you, and *three* times in the last few minutes you've stood on your right leg and

11

scratched the back of it with your left instep. No *don't* laugh. If you want to be a model my love, you've got to get out of *that* horrid little habit. I *mean*, just look at you! You're making that lovely frock look like a bit of *sea-weed*."

He flicked his hair off his forehead and started to adjust the bodice and arranged a fold in the skirt. "Sorry David," said Rachel meekly. Mrs. Kaye watched and chuckled.

"There! That's better." David was satisfied at last. "Ooh! You look *scrumptious!*" He planted a noisy kiss on her cheek and turned to Mrs. Kaye.

"Someone's going to be proud of his mum when he comes home next week. Be nice to have him working locally for a change. He'll be company for Rachel too, eh?"

He grinned at the sour look Rachel gave him, then glanced quickly round the room.

"Where's Marilyn? I haven't seen her for the last half hour."

"Oh I forgot to tell you, David," said Mrs. Kaye. "Marilyn had to leave early. She had a date with Luke. She says she will bring the frock round tomorrow morning before she goes to work."

A look of outrage swept over David's smooth face. "You *don't* mean to say she's gone riding pillion with that Hell's Angel! And in one of my frocks! Oh the *madam!*"

"David—" Mary Hornsby was smiling apologetically for the interruption. "It's been lovely. Thank you for making me come. But I really must go now. The twins —I don't like keeping the baby-sitter out late—"

"Bless you for helping out ducky. Come along, let's see if we can find someone to walk over the bridge with you. Can't let you go wandering over the river on your own."

Mary had changed out of her show gown and was wearing a light coat over a print dress. David pulled the edges of the coat together and fastened the buttons. His action was protective, almost maternal. Mary said goodnight, and with David's arm around her, walked to the door.

"It's good to see Mary coming out of her shell," said Mrs. Kaye. "She's had a rough time. Her husband was completely dependent on her for two years. I don't

13

know how she coped. And the twins are lovely. Have you seen them?"

"Yes. She often brings them to David's. He's marvellous with them. And with Mary. He won't let her wallow."

Mrs. Kaye fiddled with her bangle. "Funny how things work out. Mary was sweet on Rupert at one time, soon after they both left school. Went everywhere together. But Rupert went away to university and Mary took a secretarial course and then got a job with the Coal Board. That's where she met Richard. Poor young things. They didn't know what life had in store for them."

Do any of us? thought Rachel. Her eyes sought out Jonathan Blake.

"—of course Rupert was too interested in his studies to worry," Mrs. Kaye was saying, and Rachel smiled at the ease with which she brought the conversation round to her son.

The Rector drifted up and started talking about the Garden Fete. Rachel excused herself. Jonathan was standing alone by one of the windows. Oh if only she dared go over and speak to him—

Someone called her name softly. She

turned to find Miss Guilford, a prim, straight-backed elderly woman smiling and patting the seat next to her.

Rachel gave J.B. a lingering look before she accepted Miss Guilford's invitation and she was careful to place herself where she could watch the rest of the room.

"I would think the evening has been a success from David's point of view, wouldn't you?" asked Miss Guilford. "He's a very odd young man but so sincere one can forgive the eccentricities of his dress and speech. And of course, one is always pleased to see a local boy succeed."

Rachel watched Lena Sefton walk towards the window and J.B. "David will succeed," she said. "His designs are good and he isn't afraid of work. Doesn't Lena look marvellous? Like a tiger."

Miss Guilford's thin hand, knobbly with arthritis, moved restlessly along the arm of her chair. She looked at Lena and immediately looked away again, her mouth set in a straight line.

"Would you have tea with me one day next week, Rachel? Not a very exciting prospect for you I know but you might be interested in my photographs of Dr. Schweitzer and his clinic at Lambarene?"

Rachel who had noticed Miss Guilford's unspoken disapproval of Lena, would have done anything for her at that moment.

"Thank you. I'd love to." Her head swivelled round in a double-take. "Dr. Schweitzer? You've met him?"

"Met him? Good gracious child. I worked with him for years. I was a nurse." She held up her deformed hands. "Had to give it up."

Rachel blinked. This little old-fashioned spinster a nurse in a leper hospital! How wonderful. She thought of the girls at school. At one time, nearly all of them including Rachel herself, had romantic dreams of going out into the world to relieve suffering humanity. Dr. Schweitzer's clinic had been at the top of their list.

She looked round the room. What a waste of time all this was. How shallow now, her own ambition to be a model. With her health and strength she ought to be out there—Africa, India—wherever she was needed. She closed her eyes and her face glowed as she saw herself in clean, starched cap and apron, moving about in

16

dreadful squalor, giving a cool drink here, murmuring comforting words there—

She opened her eyes. Jonathan Blake smiled at her across the room, and Rachel's heart rocketed, plunged, and finally settled into a suffocating thump, thump, thump.

Suffering humanity was forgotten as he and Amy strolled towards her.

Amy moved with quiet assurance but her unremarkable features seemed to glow from within, her grey eyes held an expression Rachel had never seen there before. How strange! Had this man's presence stirred some chemical in the atmosphere so that people seemed brighter, more interesting? Or was she, Rachel, the only one affected? Was her own reaction making her see others more clearly?

"Rachel, I want you to meet a friend of mine, Jonathan Blake. Jonathan, this is my niece, Rachel Verity."

Jonathan's clasp was as warm and strong as she had known it would be.

"How do you do Rachel. A lovely name for a lovely child."

His small black eyes twinkled down on her and his voice had a teasing quality. His approach was so different from the one she had expected, she was unable to hide her disappointment. Child indeed!

Amy, sensing her chagrin, came to the rescue. "Rachel's just left boarding school. She's staying with me while her parents are abroad." She smiled at Rachel as she said this, then went on, "She's going to London next year. Going to be a model aren't you love?"

Rachel had been gazing at the artist but something in her Aunt's tone made her look swiftly at her. She was just in time to intercept a glance between Amy and Mrs. Kaye. An amused indulgent glance with an air of conspiracy about it. Rachel narrowed her eyes in suspicion but the two women looked at her guilelessly, and Amy said quickly, "David Ramsey lets her help him occasionally. And of course, what he can't teach her about wearing clothes—"

Suddenly David appeared, bemoaning a crisis in the kitchen. Amy and Mrs. Kaye went to deal with it.

The surprised look was still on the artist's face. "You must forgive me," he said. "I thought you were thirteen at the

18

most. Good heavens! A model! This generation seems to have been born grown up."

Rachel gave him what she imagined was a dazzling smile. "Amy has told me all about your paintings J—er Mr. Blake. I'd love to come and see them." Her voice was a fair imitation of Lena's metallic drawl.

The twinkle was replaced by a frown. "Oh call me J.B. if you want to. Everybody else does."

He looked over her head at someone and prepared to move away.

Rachel felt a terrible sense of loss. Desperately she tried to think of some gem of wit which would keep him by her side. "How long have you lived in Lynbury?" *Oh God! Why didn't the floor open and swallow her up? Of all the inane remarks!* Again, despite her anguish, her voice and manner carried faint echoes of Lena.

Another spasm of irritation drew the dark brows together. "How long—? Good Lord! I don't know. Does it matter."

His brusqueness took her breath away. She swallowed, licked her lips, stood on one leg and scratched it with her other foot, remembered David's scolding, stood

19

straight and tried not to look as miserable as she felt.

Impelled by an emotion she could neither define nor resist, though she recognised it had its quota of vanity, she tried again, hoping desperately Lena wasn't near enough to hear what a fool she was making of herself.

"I wouldn't get in your way—" Her voice was more natural but had developed a quiver. J.B. was unmoved.

"You certainly wouldn't. I wouldn't have you within a mile of me if I were busy." He gave her a straight look from his boot-button eyes. "What's all this about? Do you paint? Do you collect pictures or artists? Or what *do* you have in mind?"

His words and tone made Rachel curl up inside. She knew they were justified but shame and humiliation made her answer back.

"I don't paint. And I don't collect artists. You are the first one I've met and if they are all as rude as you, I hope you'll be the last." Tears were threatening. She did not care now, what he thought. She told him the truth. "I wanted to talk to

20

you, that's all, but I couldn't think of anything to say."

Furious with herself for the childish outburst and furious with him for the part he had played in her betrayal, she turned away.

His hands reached out and held her shoulders, drawing her back towards him. His eyes were twinkling again. "I'm sorry. I was very rude. One gets tired of silly people clacking about art, trotting out phrases they've heard on the telly—but I'm sure you aren't like that?"

"I promise not to clack, ever." The flesh of her shoulders burned from his touch but she had her voice under control, and she managed to smile naturally.

"I suppose it's flattering when people pretend to see a deeper meaning behind your paintings? Aren't they implying something? About your intelligence? I wouldn't mind them crediting me with more intelligence that I have if—oh!" She shot him a horrified look.

His head went back but his laugh was soft. Not the exhibitionist type guffaw she would have expected from most men when someone makes a *faux-pas*.

"I can see I needn't expect flattery from you, Rachel. It will be a pleasure to show you my paintings for your honest opinion only."

Rachel beamed. Lena was standing quite close, and though she seemed to be interested in what her companions were saying, she had that peculiar air of detachment people wear when they are trying to "tune in" to somebody else's conversation. As though her ears were on an extension lead, thought Rachel.

"I'm afraid my opinion isn't worth much," she said quietly to J.B. "I know nothing about art."

He smiled. "The only thing you need ask yourself when looking at a picture is, does it give *you* pleasure? If it does, it's a success as far as you are concerned. It's strictly personal." He looked from her to Lena. "That's a pretty dress you are wearing. So is the one Lena has on. But she would look insignificant in yours and you could not wear hers with the same success. David Ramsey is an artist. He has stated his point of view with those dresses. We agree with that point of view so the result pleases us."

It seemed as if by mentioning Lena's name he had conjured her up. She was by his side, her arm through his. She reached up and kissed him. "It's good to have you back darling. I'm going home. Want a lift?" Her quiet manner excluded Rachel.

"No thanks. It won't kill me to walk two hundred yards."

"See you tomorrow then?"

He nodded. Disentangled his arm and walked away. Lena turned to face Rachel. They stared at one another. Neither spoke.

David came in from the hall. "Lena, Henry says if you don't hurry he'll drive himself home. Don't let him risk it ducky. He's in no state." As Lena flounced off, he said, "Lena's a smashing driver. She's the only one I feel safe with on the road." He kissed Rachel. "Goodnight. Thanks for all your help and don't forget what I told you. Keep *both* your feet on the ground."

His tone was more significant than his words warranted and she gave him a searching look. The next moment she and Amy were carried through the front door on the tide of a laughing, noisy group.

In bed for what was left of the night,

Rachel went over in her mind the high-lights of the party, revelling in the memory of what Jonathan had said to her, trying to squeeze the last bit of meaning out of his least important remark, his every look, his every touch—

She snuggled into her pillows. Her eyes began to close. She hoped David would get his backing—fancy Miss Guilford working in a leper hospital—Lena Sefton was in love with Jonathan—Henry was jealous—had Marilyn gone pillion riding in that lovely gown?—Rupert would be home next week—

Her eyes flew open. Rupert? *Rupert*. Mrs. Kaye's son. Oh *him*. The bird-watcher. She giggled. What on earth had made her think about him?

2

"**A** PENNY for them." Amy smiled at Rachel who was dreamily taking off the top of her egg. "Did you enjoy yourself last night?"

"Mm! It had its moments." Rachel hesitated, wondering how she could bring J.B. into the conversation without arousing Amy's suspicion. "Nobody could accuse you of gossiping," she said. "I've been here a month and you've told me nothing about the natives."

"Well I dare say David has more than made up for it," said Amy, and they both laughed. "What did you want to know?"

"You could have told me about Miss Guilford working in a leper hospital. I think she's fabulous—"

"Well she's been retired a few years, and the trouble with people like her, they tend to blend into the landscape. You forget they are there until someone draws your attention to them."

"Like in a well-painted picture?" offered Rachel hopefully.

"Exactly."

When Amy didn't rise to the bait, Rachel frowned and tried again. "I'm afraid I upset Lena Sefton last night."

"Oh that wouldn't be difficult. What did you do to her?"

Rachel was silent for a moment wondering how she could explain the silly incident which had sparked off Lena's anger.

"She seemed to be warning me to keep my hands off Jonathan Blake. It was ridiculous. I hadn't even met him."

Amy reached for her coffee cup. "Oh well—she tends to regard him as her property. I expect she looks on every pretty girl as a threat to her position as his favourite model. She doesn't know you are only here for a few weeks."

Rachel's spirits drooped at the words. "Lena's jealous of her position as J.B.'s model and Henry is jealous of J.B.," she said gloomily. "It's not surprising either. It's disgusting the way she flings herself at him."

"Now Rachel."

Rachel was unrepentant. "Well she does. She did last night anyway. You should have seen poor Henry's face. I felt quite sorry for him."

"Poor Henry! Goodness me!" There was gentle mockery in Amy's voice and smile. "Why when I looked across at you, you were glaring fit to kill."

"Oh well, he'd had too much to drink and was being a bit of a bore—rocking about and raving about poisoning somebody. He said it was the only way—*oh Amy!*" A look of horror crossed her face. "You don't suppose—?"

"Suppose what?"

"Henry. He wouldn't be thinking of—" She could not finish what she had started to say.

The mockery left Amy's face. The reproof in her eyes made Rachel falter—put her on the defensive.

"Well! You should have seen the look in his eyes when J.B. came into the room and Lena latched herself onto him." Rachel paused, trying to clarify her impression. "It wasn't anger—you know —like you can get rid of in a blazing row. It was deeper than that. It sent shivers through me, honestly. I'm sure he's terribly jealous."

Amy laughed. "Lots of married couples make one another jealous. They aren't all as sophisticated as your parents." She stopped abruptly as though wondering if she had been unwise to mention that subject.

"I remember his exact words now," Rachel said cheerfully. She put down her cup, folded her napkin and stared dramatically across the table. "He said, 'Poison the blighters, it's the only way.' There! What d'you make of that?"

"Nothing." Amy began clearing the table. "You mustn't let your imagination run away with you. I've told you before. You read far too much into the things people say. You mustn't look for deeper meanings behind everything. People aren't nearly as complicated as you seem to imagine. You'll make life very difficult for yourself if you aren't careful."

"But he actually *said* that Amy. He must have meant something. I wouldn't call it a casual remark. And you should have seen his face. He was—"

"Henry's a farmer, darling." Amy

28

movements were deft and neat as she moved about the kitchen, between table and sink and the old oak dresser with its blue and white Spode and its pieces of gleaming copper. "I expect he was talking about the rats in his granary or the pigeons on his crops or something." She began running hot water into the sink. A little silence fell between them.

"Perhaps you are right," Rachel said at last. "He had been grumbling about the foxes taking his chickens. All the same—"

"You see? With an imagination like yours you should write a book."

Amy's face was bland, her smile gentle as she held out the tea-towel.

Rachel took the cloth mechanically and waited for the surplus water to drain off the cups. *Of course!* She knew Amy was joking, but what an idea! Why—she could write a fantastic book if she set her mind to it. She wouldn't have to look beyond her own experiences for material. Her own and her parents'.

She thought of Daphne and Alek Compton, the local couple who six years ago, had shared a compartment on the Britannia Express with her and her parents during a tour of Yugoslavia. After the tour the friendship had blossomed. Rachel remembered exactly when it had taken a new turn. It was during one of the Christmas holidays from school that she noticed the meaningful glances her mother had exchanged with Alek. She had sensed when her father was holding Daphne's hand under the table. She remembered writhing in embarrassment when he laughed at Daphne's feeble jokes.

Rachel had heard about defaulting parents from the girls at school and she had looked at her own with renewed interest, grateful there were no scenes, no bad temper.

She smiled to herself as she remembered how her mother had confessed to her that although she and Daddy liked one another and would always be good friends, it wasn't enough, and so darling—

The four of them had then stood in front of her, blushing and uncomfortable like naughty children brought before the headmistress.

Rachel had suppressed a giggle, congratulated them on the sensible way they had behaved and wished them happiness. The next moment they were all in a huddle, kissing, laughing, crying. At the celebration dinner that evening she had felt proud of her sophisticated and obviously happy family of four.

It was then she told them she wanted to leave school and go to London, to a modelling school, sharing a flat with two of her school chums who also wanted to be models.

She had underestimated the adults. A solid little silence had fallen, a silence more eloquent than their blank refusal.

She could leave school, yes. But London? No darling. Not for another year at least. And so they had written to Aunt Amy, Mum's sister, who had offered Rachel a temporary home until the honeymooners returned from Yugoslavia—of course—where else? The pill had been sweetened for her by the promise of a casual job with a fabulous young dress designer who lived near Amy. And here she was.

Rachel closed her eyes and thought about the book she would write. She would make it spicy. It might be a best seller—perhaps she would sell the film rights—

"Hey! Wake up!" Amy's voice entered her dream just as she was shaking hands with Prince Philip at the film premiere. Rachel was so startled she dropped the cup she was wiping.

"Oh Amy! I'm so sorry. I've spoiled your lovely set—I was miles away." She sank to her heels and began picking up the pieces.

"Careful! Don't cut yourself and don't look so tragic. It's only a cup."

Rachel stared at her. "But you treasured that set. You've had it years."

"Well that's life isn't it? Things get broken; dreams, hopes, ambitions. You pick up the pieces and carry on." She smiled and ruffled Rachel's hair. "Cheer up love. If you're going up town will you call at the greengrocers for me? And the library? I'd go myself but I want to get those cushion covers finished for the Garden Fete."

Rachel gave her a hug. "You are the kindest person I know. I hope I'm like you when I'm—" She stopped and bit her lip.

"Old?" suggested Amy.

Ten minutes later Rachel was walking across the wooden footbridge which spans the River Leen and links the old part of the village with the new or north side which is fully developed.

On her way to the traffic-free shopping precinct with its library, medical centre, post office and branch of Lloyd's Bank, Rachel passed rows of smart new bungalows with picture windows and car-ports, and gardens gay with tulips and wallflowers. There were masses of floribunda rose bushes too in whose buds chinks of yellow, red, pink or cream were showing. At regular intervals flowering cherry trees stood like pink parasols. Mary Hornsby had one in her garden. Rachel glanced in as she went by but there was no sign of either Mary or the twins.

A little further on she stopped to read the notice outside the Miners' Welfare. It offered its patrons speciality acts and comedy with their Saturday pints; vocals on Sunday; Bingo on Mondays and Tuesdays, "Beat-nite" on Wednesdays, old-tyme dancing on Thursdays and modern dancing to the Rick-Shaw Trio on Fridays.

Rachel smiled as she turned away but the smile died at the sight of the youth blocking her way. He was so close she had to step back in order not to bump into him. She had an impression of long hair, tight jeans, and white singlet.

"Hi!" he said, and smiled as though they knew one another. "What about it then? See you Wednesday night? I'll see you have a good time."

His voice was soft, insinuating; his eyes bold and his attitude so confident it was obvious to Rachel he thought he had only to ask.

She was too startled at first to do more than murmur a curt, "No thanks," and turn away.

He grabbed her arm. She looked down at his hand—big, capable, none too clean. Beautifully shaped nails rimmed with dirt.

"How about Friday then? See you outside half past eight?" His accent was flat-vowelled and careless.

"Let go my arm."

"All right. Needn't be so huffy. I only asked." He dropped his hand and stared at her, his expression a mixture of baffled

34

resentment and, she thought, genuine disappointment.

Rachel walked away to a chorus of jeers and cat-calls from the three other youths lolling on a seat outside the Welfare. Propped up against the wall were four powerful, costly-looking motor bikes.

She wondered briefly where she had seen the bold eyed youth before, then she forgot him.

Upper Lynbury was alive with children and dogs and mini-skirted housewives pushing prams and shopping trollies. It was noisy with the clanking and grinding of the colliery whose headstocks and winding gear and grassed-over spoil banks dominated the scene and served as a reminder of how the older inhabitants had earned their living.

In the greengrocers she was served by Marilyn, the girl who had defected from David's party last night. A girl whose skin was as soft and pretty as the nylon smock she wore.

Marilyn did not believe in wasting words. At least not on Rachel. She handed over the bag of onions, took the money, rang it up on the till and turned to the next customer without uttering a word.

"Excuse me! I gave you a fifty. Where's my change?" Rachel's voice was quiet but firm.

Marilyn pushed the silky blonde hair out of her eyes, took four tenpenny pieces from the till, handed them to Rachel and turned back to her other customer.

Rachel walked out of the shop bristling with indignation at the other girl's blatant attempt to cheat her.

The library opened at ten. At five past, Rachel was on her way out. Tucked under her arm was a copy of Jean Plaidy's latest historical novel, D. H. Lawrence's *Women in Love* and Noel Coward's *Private Lives*. The latter for study purposes only because Amanda and Edward reminded her so much of her own parents.

In the parking area adjoining the precinct stood Lena Sefton's yellow sports car.

Rachel looked scornful at the idea of anybody using a car to get from Lower to Upper Lynbury, for it meant a detour on to the by-pass in order to cross the river half a mile down stream. She loved to use the wooden footbridge herself; it seemed to link two different worlds.

On the way over, lingering to watch the water bubbling over the stones, she remembered where she had seen the bold eyed youth. It was down there on the triangle of meadow formed by the bridge, the river and Dark Lane, a narrow unmade road which led up to the Sefton's farm and over the hill to the woods beyond.

Three evenings ago, he had been down there kissing Marilyn. He had looked up and seen Rachel crossing the bridge, had paused in his lovemaking to wave to her. Marilyn had looked up too, then she had pushed the boy away and flounced off.

If she short-changes me again I'll jolly well go to the dance with her boy friend the next time he asks me, thought Rachel.

There was a movement in the garden of the cottage which stood on the corner of Dark Lane nearest the bridge. Miss Guilford, whom Rachel now thought of as the Lambarene nurse, waved and disappeared indoors.

A little way along the lane, standing at

right angles to it, was what had once been a barn. Painted white now, it had big windows and a skylight all facing north, looking towards the river, the bridge and Upper Lynbury.

Rachel wondered if Jonathan Blake were already at work on his portrait of Lena. And then she remembered seeing Lena's car in the precinct and the thought that she wasn't in there with him gave her a warm feeling of satisfaction.

But just in case *he* was there, and in the hope that he might just glance through his window, she draped herself gracefully against the old-fashioned lamp standard on the bridge and pretended to be admiring the higgledy-piggledy layout of the mellow stone cottages of Lower Lynbury.

After a while she wasn't seeing the old buildings. Her mind had wandered back to J.B. and his studio overlooking the river. She closed her eyes and saw herself plunging fully clothed into the water to rescue a child which had fallen in just as she, Rachel, was crossing the bridge. J.B. who had seen the heroic action from his window, came rushing out. Together they resuscitated the child and when they had seen her safely into the ambulance which another eye-witness had sent for, J.B. invited her into the studio, gave her towels and dry clothes, offered her a drink. They sat and talked—

"Rachel! Rachel!" Miss Guilford must have been watching her for some time. She was leaning on her gate and smiling.

Rachel left her day dreams on the bridge and walked towards her.

"Would you give this to David for me dear? It's the dress I wore last night."

Rachel took the long, black cardboard box with its gold imprint on one corner. "Surely Miss Guilford," said Rachel. "You looked lovely in it. David's very clever at suiting clothes to the personality, don't you think so?" She paraphrased Jonathan Blake without a blush.

Miss Guilford smiled. "His clothes certainly give one confidence in oneself. Last night I was a woman of the world in that dress." She looked down at the black and white print she now wore. "This morning I'm a dried up old spinster again."

"I don't think so. Not with all you have to look back on." Rachel smiled. "Did

39

it take an awful lot of courage to go out *there—?*"

"Not at all. One sick person is very like another. It doesn't matter where they live or what disease they are suffering from. One is glad to help. Come to tea tomorrow. Will you?"

"I'd love to. Thank you." Rachel turned at the sound of a car slowing down. Lena Sefton steered her car round the corner of the lane and drove carefully along it without a glance at either Rachel or Miss Guilford. But Jonathan Blake in the passenger seat smiled and waved.

Well! thought Rachel. All that fooling about on the bridge for his sake and he was uptown with *her*.

"See you tomorrow then dear." Miss Guilford smiled and went towards her door.

Rachel dragged her gaze away from the studio and the two people who were entering it. She juggled with her library books and dress box and her shopping bag, then walked slowly away. Crossing the road, she passed the little twelfth century church and the end of the lane which ran parallel to the Leen and on which Amy's house stood. A little further down the street she went in at a gateway belonging to one of the big Victorian houses. This one had been given a pseudo-Georgian façade. The front garden was paved over but there were several urns filled with plants. A small sign in one of the windows, in gilt lettering on black, said "David Ramsey. *Haute Couture.*"

Rachel jangled the brass bell and went in.

3

BEFORE the echo of the bell had died away Rachel had crossed the black and white tiled hall.

"Up here." The words were disembodied and indistinct. She smiled as she remembered David's cunningly placed mirrors on staircase and landing. When he was upstairs in his workroom with the door open, he could see anybody who came into the hall.

She found him on his knees fixing a length of Swiss nylon round a dressmakers' dummy. His mouth was full of pins.

Rachel put her bag of onions and her library books on a chair already piled high with copies of *Vogue* and *Flair* and scraps of material. She shook out the dress she had brought and put it on a hanger.

"Any luck last night David?"

He nodded.

"Mr. Galbraith *will* finance you? He's phoned already to say so? Oh David! How marvellous!" She looked at him closely. "You don't seem very excited."

Rachel picked up the pin box and sat cross-legged beside him. "Tell me about it."

David shrugged and shifted his position. "He wants me to move out of Lynbury. Says there isn't enough scope here."

"London?"

"Not necessarily. He thinks there'll be a gradual shift to the north. He has business interests in Newcastle. He hasn't made a definite offer but he likes my work and he made it clear he'd help in a big way if I'd be willing to move."

Rachel looked at the suits and dresses hanging round the room. "You aren't doing too badly here David. People have recommended you to their friends—you get as much work as you can cope with. What would you stand to gain?"

David gently eased a seam. "I make a good living but it's hard work on my own."

"But you take such a pride in your designs, do you really want to mass-produce them?"

"Oh it wouldn't be like that. I wouldn't

try to compete with Marks and Sparks but I'd like a small plant, a good sample hand, a few machinists and finishers. Just so that I could concentrate on designing. I'd try to remain fairly exclusive. For my Mum's sake if nothing else."

There was a silence lasting a few moments.

"But your Mum died ages ago David," Rachel spoke gently, handing him the pins as he needed them.

David reached for the scissors and trimmed off a surplus half inch of material. He pushed his fair hair off his forehead. It was several seconds before he spoke.

"You'll never know what it cost her to put me through Art School. Not in cash but in moral courage. We lived uptown in a grubby little terrace house, two up and two down. Shared lavatory in the back yard. Washing strung across the street. Every male between fourteen and sixty-five worked at the pit. Had their names put down as soon as they were born. Like Eton. Poor devils."

"And your Mum wanted something better for you?"

"She did. And when Lynbury top pit flooded and took my dad, that was it as far as she was concerned. Any way I'd always been different." He laughed unself-consciously. "I expect I was the result of her deep longing for a daughter. Didn't quite make it, poor old love. My, but she had something to put up with from the neighbours."

He stood up and stretched himself. "So you see ducky. Can't let Mum down." He brushed at the pieces of nylon thread sticking to his dark blue velvet pants and jerked at the frilly cuff of his pale blue shirt. He laughed. "One side effect of it was, I learned to use my fists. Surprise, surprise!" He flexed his muscles. "Had to. Couldn't get in our back yard without flat-tening a few of the neighbours' kids first. My great-uncle Alfred taught me. He was the local champ. Used to box at Goose Fair—you know—he got a pound for every round he could stay on his feet against their champ. My *word* but I've been grateful to him!"

David laughed and pretended to spar with Rachel. He dropped his fists.

"Rupert's pretty handy with his left hook too," he said.

"Rupert?"

"Rupert Kaye."

"Oh *him*. The birdwatcher." Her voice dropped several semitones.

"Don't be like that," David lisped effeminately. In his normal tone he said, "You'll like Rupert. Everybody does."

That's enough to put me off, thought Rachel. But she hadn't sufficient interest in him to argue the point.

She was wondering if she dared introduce the subject of J.B. Unlike Amy, David loved a good old gossip. His workroom was often filled with chattering women. It seemed to have taken the place of the village post-office. They would come in to ask David's advice about a pattern or material, or to be fitted for a garment which was already in hand, and they would stay to air their grievances, knowing full well that however many times David had heard the story or one of its variations, he would be ready with a cluck of sympathy or a murmur of surprise. And he never gave advice unless he was sure

46

his advice went along the lines they already intended to follow. This rule was broken only when people he cared for were involved. Like Rachel.

He knew whose husband was reputedly "having a bit on the side"; which wife was discontented because her husband was too tired to take her dancing, yet came wide awake the minute they got in bed. (If he heard the woman's husband complaining over a pint in the local that his wife was frigid, David kept his own counsel.) If an incident wasn't talked about in his workroom it hadn't happened. "I heard it at David's" was a seal of authenticity.

"Lena Sefton's pretty chummy with our resident artist," Rachel said flippantly, without looking at him.

"Now *there's* a girl who knows how to wear clothes," said David, side-stepping neatly, so that Rachel could not tell if it was a deliberate evasion. "*She* wouldn't dream of scratching herself in public. Not like some people I could mention."

"Oh David!" Rachel protested. But she had no intention of being diverted. "I think she looked magnificent last night. She reminded me of Blake's '*Tyger*'."

Somehow, despite her air of non-chalance, the name seemed to come out in capital letters. David shot her a look. She gazed back innocently.

"No wonder he's painting her portrait."

Immediately she had said it, confusing the two Blakes, she felt she had given herself away. She could almost feel the thoughts transferring themselves from his brain to hers and back again. Her face flamed.

Damn his feminine intuition, she thought, little realising it was her candid, ever-changing face which told its own story.

"Quite a heart-throb isn't he?" said David. "Don't get carried away ducky. Lena wouldn't like it. Haven't you noticed the keep-off signs? The way she shoots barbed wire out of her eyes if another woman goes near him?"

Rachel snorted, half in amusement at the apt description, half in anger.

"What's it got to do with her? She's only his model. She doesn't own him. Anyway she's married." Rachel began sorting out a box of remnants, cutting up small pieces, folding up anything which might be useful.

David stood up, flexed his knees, moved round the back of the dummy and spoke to Rachel over its shoulder.

"She doesn't own him but she owns his studio. And she makes sure he doesn't forget it."

Rachel pouted. "Well—he must pay rent. Surely she couldn't turn him out even if she wanted to? I mean, it's his home isn't it? Not just where he paints?"

"Peppercorn."

"What?"

"Peppercorn. He pays her a peppercorn rent. The studio was a ramshackle old barn when he took it over. It was agreed verbally that if he restored it at his own expense he could use it for as long as he paid a peppercorn rent and the rates. But the arrangement was made with Henry. He and J.B. were quite pally in those days."

"And now?"

"Now," David unpinned something, refolded it and pinned it up again. "Well now property prices have rocketed. That studio is worth a packet. So is the land it stands on. Even if it were sold as a single plot, going down to the river as it does, it would fetch a thousand or two. But Henry wants to sell the whole lot to the developers. The farm, the bridge, everything. There's about a hundred and thirty acres all together."

"For a housing estate?" Rachel looked horrified.

David nodded. "Awful thought ain't it? Actually, they want to build a proper bridge in place of the wooden one. Widen the road and make Upper and Lower Lynbury into one big town. Henry stands to make a bomb."

"Oh it's too ghastly! This lovely village? Miss Guilford's cottage with its thatched roof? Amy's pretty house too? They'd all be destroyed. Is that what they want? What about the people?"

"People aren't allowed to stand in the way of progress ducky. People don't matter any more. Not individuals. The powers that be will always argue that what they do is for the benefit of the majority."

Rachel was silent for a while, pushing the pins around in the pin-box, creating little patterns, disturbing them and creating others.

"If Henry wants to sell to the developers what's stopping him?" she asked when the silence had gone on a long time.

"Lena. You see, in order to avoid death duties, Henry gave some of the land to her. Deed of gift. Loving care and affection—all that piece of land and the buildings thereon. She owns the meadow, Miss Guilford's cottage, the foot-bridge too, I believe, and the studio."

David bent down, adjusted something, bobbed up again and met Rachel's eyes squarely. "That wasn't enough for Lena. She wanted J.B. as well."

"How long is it since Henry transferred the land?"

"About two years. And J.B. transferred his friendship from Henry to Lena about the same time. He hadn't much use for her until then."

"He doesn't seem to have much use for her now," said Rachel, remembering the artist's off-hand manner with Lena at the party last night. "Except as a model."

"He's a little more discreet in public than she is perhaps."

"I expect she blackmailed him into painting her portrait. That's what happened?" She looked at David for confirmation. He was too busy to answer.

"You'd think he'd have some rights to the studio after spending time and money on it. Couldn't a solicitor—?"

"Jonathan Blake doesn't need a solicitor to sort things out for him. He does all right. Take it from me. He—"

"David! What are you suggesting. As if I didn't know."

"Who—me? I'm not suggesting anything."

"You think they are lovers? Right under Henry's nose?"

David hesitated. "You know how people talk," he said. Again he gave her a straight look. "In Lynbury everybody knows everybody else's business. It's impossible to keep *anything* secret. In my opinion if people don't want to get themselves talked about they shouldn't do silly things."

He's talking *at* me, Rachel thought. He's warning me. She picked up a copy of *Vogue* and flipped through the pages.

"People can be wrong you know, David. Everybody accuses everybody else of doing what they themselves would do in the same circumstances. They could be wrong."

David didn't seem to have heard. "You know," he said dreamily, "I've often wondered if Lena would have looked at him twice if he hadn't been an artist. I mean, if he'd been a butcher, or a miner, or a chap in an office or a factory."

Rachel knew what he was hinting at and she pretended to be absorbed in an advertisement.

"Have you seen his portrait of her? No of course you won't have—"

"He's invited me round to the studio. I'll go when I have nothing better to do." She put down the magazine and stared through the window at the flagged square below. "If it's true what people say, surely Henry would have divorced her by now?" said Rachel to whom divorce was a fact of life.

David shook his head. "The Seftons are Catholics. No divorce." He picked up the dummy and carried it to the wall. "There! Got it right at last." He stood back and looked admiringly at his handiwork. "That's pretty good though I say it myself.

Even if Henry divorced her, J.B. would never marry Lena. He's not the marrying kind."

Rachel blinked at David's quick change of subject. "How do you know?"

"I know that anybody as possessive and demanding as Lena would be the kiss of death to any artist. What about some coffee ducky?"

Rachel put coffee into an earthenware jug and brought out two huge cups.

"J.B. can't stand children," said David. "Not like me. I love it when Mary brings the twins here. He plays hell with Lena when her little boy goes anywhere near the studio."

"Well. Just because he doesn't like children and possessive women, doesn't mean he's a confirmed bachelor. Perhaps if the *right* woman came along?"

"There's no such thing now. He's too set in his ways. Look Rachel my love, there are two sorts of people, the givers and the takers. J.B. is a taker. So is Lena in a different way. They understand each other. Each knows how far to go, what to expect from the other. They'll never do one another any harm. But you now, just supposing you were stupid enough to lose your head to someone like him, his type, but *younger*." He gave her his wide-eyed stare before which she lowered her own eyes. "It would be fatal. You are a giver. You'd give till it hurt, if I'm not mistaken and you'd get nothing in return. Nothing worth having."

He took the coffee Rachel held out to him and spooned crystals into it. "I bet when one of his pictures turns out as he wants it to, he wouldn't change places with Aristotle Onassis."

"And when things go wrong?"

David laughed. "I know what you're thinking but it's not like that in real life. So think twice before you offer yourself up as a sacrifice. Or a door-mat. And now! Let's stop talking twaddle. I don't know how we got on to such a silly subject."

Rachel sipped her coffee. "I think it's terrible the way people tear reputations to shreds. Lena ought to be—"

David, who had been watching her with troubled eyes said quickly. "Oh Lena will survive. And however much the natives disapprove, they know that but for her the bull-dozers would be in."

"I wasn't thinking of Lena. She has a husband to protect her." Rachel looked up in alarm as David spluttered. "What's wrong?"

David choked back his laughter. He was saved the bother of a reply as an internal door banged and footsteps sounded on the stairs. Rachel looked in the mirror and watched a plump, untidy woman approaching the workroom.

"Come in Mrs. Jakes," called David. She came in, looked at Rachel and nodded. The movement dislodged an inch of ash hanging from her cigarette.

"I've finished downstairs David. I'll do your bedroom tomorrow. I'm going up-town. Want anything bringing?"

David looked at the ash on the floor. "One of these days you'll send us up in flames," he said. "How many times have I got to tell you to put out your cigarette before you come in here?"

"Sorry. I forgot." But Mrs. Jakes made no attempt to get rid of the cigarette which stuck to her bottom lip and wagged about as she spoke. "They've picked up Marilyn's brother again, did you know? Miners' Welfare. Got in through a window at the back same as last time. And *she's* no better than she ought to be. Out with that Luke till the early hours. Him and his motor bike polluting everything. Did you say you didn't want anything bringing?"

"No thanks Mrs. Jakes. Mary Hornsby's doing my shopping for me."

"Urr, she is, is she? Urr well." Mrs. Jakes managed to look offended. Another lump of ash fell but David had his back turned. She rubbed it into the floor with her foot.

"Jonathan Blake was in a paddy this morning. Young Nicholas Sefton put a ball through his studio window. Had to go uptown for glass and putty." She chuckled and her fat chins wobbled. "Sometimes I think that child goes out of his way to torment him. Serve him right, randy old devil."

She glanced at Rachel just in time to catch the tail end of a glare. Rachel turned away, and so missed the eloquent raising of Mrs. Jakes's eyebrows. The woman drew heavily on her cigarette, her small downward slanting eyes almost disappearing into the folds of the lids as she screwed them up against the smoke. She spoke softly to David.

David's face was expressionless. "Oh Rachel doesn't know who you're talking about. I doubt if they've even met."

"Urr well, she wants to watch out for him when she does meet him. Randy old devil." Mrs. Jakes repeated the last three words in a tone of voice which invited comment. David was game.

"Ooh Mrs. Jakes! You *don't* mean to say he's made a pass at you? Well I *never!*" His voice was as shrill as he could make it.

Mrs. Jakes stretched her lips in what could be described as a grim smile but did not answer. She let her silence speak for itself and seemed satisfied at the startled look on Rachel's face.

"Oh go *on*. I'll bet you encouraged him, you sex bomb you." He gave her fat behind a slap and held the door open invitingly.

Mrs. Jakes chuckled her way to the door. "Urr well! Got to get on. I can't hang about all day long doing nothing. Not like some people."

Neither David nor Rachel spoke until

they heard her footsteps clatter across the tiled floor below.

"Urr well," said David. "Open the window ducky. Let out the fug."

Rachel did as she was asked then turned to David who was stitching a seam with long, even threads, removing pins as he did so.

"David," she went over to him, and dropped the pins in the box. "A few moments ago, you said something about if I were *stupid* enough to fall in love with a man like J.B.—"

She was aware of his look though she kept her own eyes averted.

"What I mean is—you can't help falling in love can you? You don't choose. It just happens, surely?"

David sewed a few more stitches. "You *can* choose. Right at the beginning. It's easy then. But once the ball starts to roll down hill—" He shrugged. "Mind you, I don't think you're in any danger of falling in love with the wrong type. You seem a nice, sensible, well brought up young lady to me. Good stable background—"

59

He spoke the last words without thinking, then broke off, confused.

Rachel stared at him and burst out laughing.

4

RACHEL, on her way to tea with Miss Guilford, had just turned the corner by the church when ahead of her she saw a trim figure in cream pants and orange and purple tunic. Mrs. Kaye was pushing a shopping trolley as well as carrying her basket. Rachel ran and caught up with her.

"Hello Rachel." Mrs. Kaye turned at the sound of her approach. "Oh what a pretty dress. What there is of it." They both laughed and Mrs. Kaye went on, "I was thinking how lucky you and Amy are, having the pool at the bottom of the garden. We laughed at her when she spent all that money on having her little bit of the Leen deepened and the sides concreted, but my goodness, we envy her, this weather."

"But I've heard Amy tell you to use it whenever you want."

"Yes, I know. I burn too easily though. Still, I like to sit and watch her. She's a

61

lovely swimmer. Can't do much in a small pool like that of course—When she was younger she'd have reached championship class if it hadn't been for that crotchety old father of hers. Such a pity when children have to sacrifice their ambitions for the sake of their parents. And not only their ambitions—"

She stopped as though she thought she had said too much.

Rachel's memory stirred. Amy talking about the broken cup. "Things get broken —dreams, hopes, ambitions. You pick up the pieces and carry on." The glow on her face when she was with J.B. at the party. Amy and J.B.? She dismissed the idea as ridiculous. It must have been the wine. But he *had* kissed her. Was he in love with her? Had he ever painted Amy's portrait?

Rachel admired her Aunt enormously. Without shedding any of her femininity, she was completely emancipated. With her clubs and committees, her visits to the theatre and concert hall, her many friends of both sexes, she didn't seem to be missing out on life at all.

She thought of all the gossip she had

heard at David's. Never anything about Amy. Perhaps Mrs. Kaye—

"This is a gossipy village isn't it? The things you hear at David's. I was wondering if Amy—?"

Mrs. Kaye had already forgotten her remarks about Amy and was totally unaware of the thoughts they had sparked off. Rachel's question had interrupted a flow of Rupertisms. Now Rachel smiled at her. A warm, confiding smile. A clear invitation to add to and condone the gossip.

"Oh it's no worse than in any other small community," said Mrs. Kaye. "And providing you don't repeat what you hear, there's always an element of pleasure to be had listening to other people's misfortunes."

Rachel fidgeted under the slight snub, the cool stare and her own frustration. Mrs. Kaye was as bad as any of them when they were all together in the workroom, she remembered. What she did not realise was that the older woman's fastidiousness would not allow her to jump the generation gap.

All the same, when Mrs. Kaye smiled at her disarmingly, she grinned back. "I'm looking forward to meeting Rupert. Again," she added hastily.

"You must ask him to teach you how to swim."

Rachel looked at her in alarm.

"I've seen you flapping about in the water. You're a disgrace. Didn't they teach you to swim at school?"

Rachel shuddered at the abortive attempts and her eventual renunciation in favour of long country walks.

"To tell you the truth, I'm *terrified* of water. I can't bear it when my face goes under. If Rupert or anybody else comes within touching distance of me when I'm in the pool, I'll die of fright. I know I will. I'll just die."

She looked so panic-stricken Mrs. Kaye laughed.

And the child who was to be so dramatically rescued from the river under the admiring gaze of Jonathan Blake?

The nice thing about daydreams is that they can be arranged to suit the dreamer. Rachel could provoke crises and conjure up miracles merely by closing her eyes. Some were more feasible than others.

"Mrs. Kaye—you know the lane that

runs by the side of the river up to the Sefton's farm—?"

"Dark Lane?"

"Yes. Well—I was wondering what would happen if the Seftons' bull got out. Little children—you know—"

"The Seftons' bull? Do they have one?"

"Doesn't every farmer?"

"I doubt it these days. Only on mixed farms. Henry concentrates on cereals."

Rachel sighed heavily. "I'm relieved to hear it."

They had reached Miss Guilford's gate. "What was all that in aid of?" asked Mrs. Kaye as Rachel opened the garden gate.

"Oh nothing. Amy's trying to persuade me to write a book. I think I will."

"Do. I can't wait to read it."

Miss Guilford's keen blue eyes seemed to notice everything from the shortness of Rachel's frock to the dumbfounded look on her face as she watched Jonathan Blake walk away from the back door of the cottage, down the garden path between the plum and apple trees, towards his own studio.

"Mr. Blake often pops in for a chat and

a cup of tea," she explained. "But I thought it would be nicer if there were just the two of us." She looked at the firm young face tinted by the sun, the dark, expressive eyes, the long, long legs. "You are very pretty Rachel. I wouldn't be surprised if he wants to paint your portrait."

"Oh that would be fun." Rachel's voice gave no indication of the excitement she felt at Miss Guilford's words. "But I'm only here for a week or two so I don't suppose there'll be time."

The cottage was small but charming; the furniture old-fashioned and pleasantly irregular. The tablecloth was lace and the cups and saucers decorated with a delicate Chinese design. A big bow window overlooked the garden and the willows at the river's edge.

On a desk were several photos of Miss Guilford with groups of smiling nurses. There were other photographs of an elderly man mostly in the company of animals.

"Dr. Schweitzer," said Miss Guilford, following Rachel's glance. She began to talk about the Doctor and his work in

Lambarene. Rachel listened fascinated as she sipped her tea and ate the wafer-thin sandwiches and the biscuits and cake which were offered with such old world graciousness.

No wonder J.B. likes coming here, she thought. It's so restful. Like living in another age.

"I could have married," Miss Guilford was saying, "but I knew I could never have children. And if there were to be no children I couldn't see the point of tying myself down to a man and a few sticks of furniture." She smiled and reached for Rachel's cup. "Of course, it was nice to know my little home was waiting for me whenever I wanted to return."

There was a sparkle in her eye which seemed to Rachel to say a good deal more than her words.

"I'm not a great believer in marriage myself," said Rachel, picking out those remarks which were relevant to her own desires. "I think it's possible to enjoy the companionship of the opposite sex— without all that."

Miss Guilford looked pained as though realising she had given the wrong impression. Fortunately she was unaware of the seed she had planted in her young visitor's mind. A mind made receptive by David Ramsey's remark the previous day that "J.B. will never marry Lena or anybody else. He's not the marrying kind." Perhaps not, but he evidently likes a few home comforts, thought Rachel.

"Surely *you* hope to have children, Rachel?"

"I've never thought about it. I suppose that means I'm not bothered one way or the other. I mean—if I fell in love with a man who didn't want children either because he didn't like them or because he was dedicated to his ar—his work, I wouldn't mind not having them."

There was a little smiling silence as they watched the bluetits swinging upside down on a piece of suet in a mesh bag hanging from one of the apple trees. A starling trying a similar acrobatic act, made a complete fool of himself.

"Fascinating creatures aren't they?" Miss Guilford said. "I'm so glad that at last more people are taking an interest in our wild-life."

Look out! Here comes Rupert! thought

68

Rachel irritably. But she relaxed when her hostess said, "I hear you are hoping to go to London. To become a model? What are you doing meanwhile? I'm sure there isn't much work for you at David Ramsey's. Aren't you bored?"

Rachel felt guilty. What Miss Guilford really meant was "Fancy a healthy young girl like you wasting her life in this rustic backwater."

"I'd thought of writing a book." She laughed self-consciously. "I know it sound conceited but I was pretty good at writing essays at school and—" She broke off, wondering why, in spite of her charm, Miss Guilford made her feel so inadequate.

"You had eh?" There wasn't a hint of amusement in the old lady's face. "What would it be about?"

"Oh—I haven't made up my mind yet. I know a lot of interesting people but I think it will mostly be about my parents. They're fabulous."

Miss Guilford's expression was hard to read. After a moment or two she said gently, "Don't waste too much time thinking about it dear. Get something down on paper, and if I can be of any help—"

"You?" Rachel looked confused. "I'm sorry. I didn't mean to sound so surprised. Do you mean—you are a writer as well as everything else?"

Miss Guilford smiled and pointed to the bookcase. Rachel went over and inspected the titles. There were six under the name of Elizabeth Guilford.

"Well of all things! May I?" She looked across at the author.

"Of course."

Rachel took down the books. Four were travel and adventure stories, two were hospital romances.

"Well!" Rachel said again. "How on earth did you find time to do this as well as your work at the hospital?"

"Positive thinking." Miss Guilford was smiling but her voice was firm. "You can do anything if you set your mind to it. Anything at all. Within reason of course. But it's no good saying 'I wish I could do this' or 'I'd like to do that'. The thing to do is say to yourself, 'I'm going to do it and nothing will stop me'. Then get on with it. Don't let the thought that you might not succeed ever enter your head."

"Oh I think you are a marvellous person."

"Borrow the books if you like."

"Thank you. I'll take great care of them." Rachel hesitated, feeling full of a gratitude she could not quite understand. An overwhelming sense of gratitude which had nothing to do with the loan of six books. Positive thinking! *I will!*

Miss Guilford smiled. "And now, let me show you round the garden."

To Rachel's delight, as they sauntered down the path, stopping here and there to admire a velvet-faced pansy, the intricate design of the aquilegias, the bed of yellow irises, Jonathan Blake came and stood in the doorway of his studio and waved.

Please, *please* come and talk to us. Rachel "willed" him as hard as she could but after a moment or two he went in.

To Rachel it was as if the sun had gone behind a cloud, yet she was conscious of a lingering warmth.

As they turned towards the house she said, "Who lives in the cottage on the opposite corner to you? I'm sure somebody is watching us through the curtains."

"Oh that will be Mrs. Jakes. All my guests are subject to her scrutiny. She's a terrible gossip—it's a good job I'm an old woman or I don't know what she would make of Mr. Blake's visits. But one mustn't be too critical, I expect she's lonely. Sad to have reached her age and to have nothing on which to look back. Still, she's a very useful person as both David and Mr. Blake have found out. She cleans for them. Mr. Blake for one, would be lost without her."

Rachel was amazed at the sharp pang of jealousy which shot through her. At the same time, her brain recorded the fact that J.B. was not the completely independent type David had made him out to be.

"Well my dear—" Miss Guilford put a small bunch of lilies of the valley into Rachel's hand. "It's been lovely talking to you. You will come again?"

Rachel looked over her shoulder towards the studio. "I certainly will. Thank you for asking me. And for *everything*."

Back in her room she opened the window wide and sat with her elbows on the sill, her chin cupped in her hand, looking in the direction of the cottage.

Positive thinking. Deliberately, she conjured up a picture of Jonathan Blake. The small, bird-like eyes, the bony nose, the bright silver hair—oh if only—

"I will. I will. I *will*," she said aloud.

5

RACHEL tucked the tickets into her bag and walked along the forecourt of the Nottingham Playhouse where lunchtime drinkers sat under brightly coloured umbrellas.

Rounding the corner by the Albert Hall she waited for the traffic lights turn to green. Her thoughts were on Jonathan Blake as usual. And suddenly, there he was, walking down the hill on the other side of the road. She thought her imagination had conjured him up. A figure made familiar because it filled all her dreams and waking thoughts.

He hadn't seen her. She crossed the road and followed him. When he entered the pedestrian subway, she sped round the corner of Parliament Street, crossed the road, doubled back and entered the subway from the opposite direction.

Breathlessly she confronted him. "Hello," she said. "What a surprise!"

They stared at one another, his face

grave, hers flushed, her eyes starry. Now that she was face to face with him, she could think of nothing to say.

"Good morning er—Rachel!" His expression was kind but he had almost forgotten her name! She stared at him in dismay. He couldn't have! He had been in her thoughts so much she couldn't, she *wouldn't* believe he had not been thinking of her too.

Was it part of his technique? A show of indifference? To make her keener? Yes, that was it!

He was waiting for her to speak, but again, as at the party, she was tongue-tied. He waited a little longer then they both spoke together.

"Are you doing a little shopping?"

It was ludicrous they should have used identical words. Such banal ones at that, but they gave Rachel her cue.

"I've been buying theatre tickets for this evening. It's Amy's birthday. We're going out to dinner first." Oh if only he would come too! "Why not come and have a drink with us before we go?" The invitation was issued before the thought was properly formulated.

75

"Thank you. I'd be delighted." He hesitated, then said, "Rachel, if you aren't in a hurry will you do something for me?"

"Oh *yes. Anything*," she answered faintly but fervently.

He looked amused. "Well then, come and help me choose a present for Amy."

"I'd love to." Why, he was practically one of the family! "I know exactly what she wants—" She stopped, confused.

"Yes?"

"Well, it's a book. An autobiography. But it's four pounds." She looked at him anxiously.

He laughed outright, took hold of her arm, and she knew he must have felt the shiver of ecstasy which ran through her.

"Come along, let's get out into the sunshine. Four pounds eh?" He smiled down at her as they reached pavement level. "That should leave me with just enough to buy you a cup of coffee. I can't offer you lunch. I have someone coming at one-thirty."

Rachel pushed away the thought that it was probably Lena Sefton, and concentrated on the other things J.B. had just said. "That should leave me with just enough to buy you a cup of coffee—I can't offer you lunch." Her mind linked the two statements and rejected the reason he had offered.

Wasn't it a fact that artists and writers had a struggle to make ends meet? This could be the reason for his dependence on Lena. Should she offer to pay for coffee? Within seconds she was imagining herself sacrificing her career to his. She would give up the idea of modelling. Instead, she would get David to show her how to use a sewing machine. According to the advertisement a machinist in a factory could earn thirty pounds a week—she leaned protectively towards him.

"You are very quiet, Rachel. Are you sure I'm not imposing on you?"

"Of course not."

She was in her seventh heaven of delight as they walked down to Sisson and Parkers' bookshop on Wheeler Gate. No need to rack her brains now, to think of something to say. It was enough just to *be*.

She became aware of his puzzled look. "Weren't you going in the opposite direction to me in the subway?"

The question startled her. The guilty colour flooded her cheeks.

He eyed her suspiciously. "Don't tell me you were lost down there? I thought it was only old squares like me who couldn't adjust to subterranean life."

"You're not an old square." Rachel was on the point of adding something rather unwise, but a woman with a pram and three whining children came charging along the pavement, forcing them apart. The woman was yelling at the children to "Be quiet will you!" There was a raised hand, the sound of a slap and more yells as they went on their way.

"Oh the joys of married life!" said Jonathan.

Rachel smiled. The time was not yet ripe for argument.

After Amy's present had been bought they browsed around the shop, discussing authors, examining books on art. Rachel knew she would treasure the memory of this morning until the day she died.

They went for coffee to a tiny place off Long Row. "Why, this looks like something straight out of Dickens," said Rachel, looking at the bow-windowed shops in the alley. In the restaurant, she fell in love with the oak beams, and revelled in the intimacy of small tables in dimly lighted corners.

"This is Amy's favourite, and mine," said Jonathan.

The pause before the last two words prevented the fusion of the two statements into one idea. Rachel felt she could not have borne it if he had said "It's *our* favourite." As it was, she wondered why Amy had never brought her here.

"Be with you in a minute Mr. Blake." A passing waitress smiled.

"Hm! Friends in high places I see," said Rachel when coffee was served. "Those people in the corner were before us."

He didn't answer and she felt terrible, wondering if he had taken her remarks as an implied criticism. That worry was forgotten as she discovered another one. Her throat made a terrible noise when she swallowed the coffee. She tried taking small sips, she tried drinking deeply. It made no difference. J.B. was frowning and drumming his fingers on the table. Rachel nearly choked in her agony.

Suddenly the small eyes started to

twinkle. "I forgot to buy a sketching block. Another sign of advancing age."

"Nonsense!" Rachel forgot her noisy throat. "Artists and writers are always absent-minded."

"Do you know any writers?" His smile couldn't have been more friendly.

"None." Treacherously, she dismissed Miss Guilford. She did not want to talk about her just now.

His smile faded slightly. "And you told me at the party the other night that you don't know any artists. Apart from me?" It was a question rather than a statement.

Rachel blushed furiously. The implication irritated her despite the justice of it.

"I don't, but I've read about them lots of times." Oh God! How childish he made her feel!

He stretched out his hand and touched her fingers. His touch, brief as it was, set her quivering. She could hardly control the violence of her feelings which his action provoked. It was is if he had turned on a switch and released in her an emotion she could not recognise and therefore could not discipline.

"Don't believe all you hear, Rachel

dear. Live your own life and draw your own conclusions."

She tried to control her trembling hands, failed, and sat on them. She drew a deep breath and when she was sure of her voice asked him, "Do you ever work out of doors or do you only paint portraits?"

"I think I've painted every corner of Lynbury that's worth painting. But my favourite place is Derbyshire. There is nothing to equal the soft beauty of those hills and dales and the beautiful wrinkled streams. Do you know Derbyshire?"

"Parts of it." Rachel smiled, feeling at ease now, hugging to herself the knowledge of something she had done last year. An achievement of which she was proud. But she wouldn't tell him until she knew him better. Wouldn't he be surprised! Everybody else had been. Mum, Dad, her new step-parents. She had gone with an organised party of course and finished up with septic blisters but she had done it. She had walked the Pennine Way from Edale to Kirk Yetholm! She could hardly believe it herself now.

She sat smiling to herself, imagining the

admiration and amazement which would spread over his face when she told him.

"I spend a lot of time up there," J.B. was saying. "I used to prefer the moors of course, the bleak, wild beauty and the cloud patterns racing over the emptiness." He sighed. "Unfortunately the damned place is like Piccadilly Circus now, since the hikers discovered the Pennine Way. Everybody, little kids and their grannies seem to be walking to Scotland. I don't know why they do it, do you? Masochists, the lot of 'em."

Bleakly, Rachel groped for her bag. She felt like a dried up old stick. "I think I ought to be going."

He looked at her then. It was the first time he had really looked at her since they met. She could tell by his expression that he was wondering what he had said to upset her. She felt him groping for words with which to cheer her up again. He asked about her parents, was she missing them?

"Good heavens no. You seem to forget I'm not a child. Lots of girls are married and have babies by the time they are my age."

"More's the pity." As he spoke, he signalled to a passing waitress. She put down a plate of Danish pastries in front of Rachel who was as indignant as if he had offered her a lollipop.

"Oh no! Not for me, thank you."

"I can thoroughly recommend them and you could do with a bit more padding."

Well if he thought that, she was prepared to eat the lot.

Cheerful again, and remembering Lena's fleshy hips she asked, "Do you like well padded women?"

He smiled but his manner was less personal now she had ceased to be upset. "I like women. All shapes and sizes, all colours and creeds. All I ask is that they smell nice."

The words had a familiar ring. Rachel wondered where she had heard them before. But the answer satisfied her. It was honest. It seemed to hint at past adventures and to hold out a promise for the future. Her future. She would make it so by positive thinking.

"What are you and Amy going to see tonight?"

"It's a play by David Storey. I like his

books don't you? They are very honest. He doesn't leave much to the imagination."

"You think Amy will enjoy it?"

Rachel laughed. "I think so. She nearly refused to go when I told her it was described as 'Naturalistic'. She wanted to know if it meant it was the sort of play where the actors take off all their clothes."

She was trying to show him how broad-minded and adult she was, but he was looking at his watch and fidgeting.

She wiped her lips on her napkin and prepared herself to leave as soon as he was ready.

"I have ten minutes in which to catch my bus," he told her as they got up to go.

"What a pity I'm not seventeen. Amy's going to teach me to drive her car if I'm still with her—" She looked at him to see what effect her impending departure had on him. He did not seem to have heard.

"Don't you drive Jonathan?" (If everybody else called him J.B. *she* would call him Jonathan.)

"No. I failed my test three times and my car was always showing me up for the mechanical fool I am, so I got rid of it.

Well Rachel—" He smiled, dismissing her.

She took the hint, denying herself the pleasure of travelling home on the same bus as him.

"Thank you for the coffee." She half turned away, then, unable to stop herself, she turned back. "It was *lovely* meeting you."

There must have been something odd in her voice because he looked at her curiously for a moment or two before he said, "You are a funny child." And as she began walking away, he added, "Would you like to come into Derbyshire with me the next time I go? We'll talk to Amy about it, shall we?"

The world seemed to spin around her. Resisting a desire to watch him until he was out of sight, she turned and walked— floated, in the opposite direction.

Rachel went home on the local bus which meandered through the lanes and finished its journey in Upper Lynbury.

The boy who had spoken to her outside the Miners' Welfare a few days ago was lolling against the lamp post on the bridge.

Luke. Marilyn's boy friend. He was wearing a singlet of washed-out blue cotton which set off the brown of his face and arms. His jeans were blue, too, with darker patches roughly sewn.

"Hi! Knew I'd catch you if I waited long enough." He stood astride the narrow bridge, blocking her way. His dark, shoulder-length hair lifted in the breeze. His teeth, strong and white gleamed in a friendly grin.

This boy would be a wow on the pop scene, thought Rachel. He has a touch of the Humperdincks with Tom Jones thrown in for good measure. She could understand his success with girls but he did not attract her.

"How about it then? Made up your mind?"

"About what?"

"Dance at th'Welfare. You'd enjoy it. I'm best dancer there is round here. Ask anybody." He danced a few intricate and graceful steps on the bridge.

"*Sur le Pont*—" Rachel sang softly. "Shall I ask Marilyn?"

"Oh her! Is that what's botherin' you? You don't have to worry about her."

"I wasn't." Rachel looked across the meadow to the studio. For a moment she forgot Luke and was taken completely off guard when he put his arms round her and tried to kiss her.

She struggled free and lashed out at him with clenched fists, arms flailing like the sails of a windmill, hating his touch and the thought that they could be seen from the studio, "How *dare* you!" She was panting with rage. "If you ever do that again I'll—" But she was so angry and humiliated she hardly knew what to threaten him with.

Luke grinned. "Aye! You don't half play hard to get." Then he began to sulk. "P'raps you think you're too good for me. Is that it? Stuck up little cow! You'll come runnin' afore I ask you again."

He slouched away and stood glaring at her from a distance of a few yards. Rachel picked up the parcels she had dropped when he grabbed her.

As she replaced them in her shoulder bag he called out, "I'll give Marilyn the push if you want me to."

She refused to answer. Refused to look at him. As she left the bridge she heard him clattering after her and she recoiled, expecting another attack. He jumped in front of her and held out a long, narrow packet.

"You dropped your paint brushes."

Their eyes met. "Artist are you? Like him?" he jerked his head in the direction of the studio.

Rachel gave him a haughty look and turned away. The boy loped along by her side.

"I didn't mean any harm duck. Honest. I wouldn't hurt a fly. I could go for you. You the best lookin' dolly we ever had round here. Marilyn's not bad but she can't hold a candle to you. You talk nice. You dress nice an' you got smashing legs."

Rachel drew a sharp breath. She didn't want this boy's compliments. Didn't want him to admire her—and yet—how nice it was to be chased instead of having to do the chasing! Suddenly she laughed.

"That's more like it," said Luke. "Does that mean you'll come? To th'Welfare? I'll get there early and get a table but don't keep me waiting else somebody else might run off wi' me."

Rachel fought back a rising fit of the

giggles. "No, I'm sorry Luke. I can't come." Her curiosity got the better of her. "Haven't you got a job?"

His face lit up as though he thought he had discovered a reason for her stand-offishness.

"Of course I have. I'm on nights though. Reg'lar. I make a lot of money." He nodded towards his motor bike leaning against the scarred old tree between the bridge and Miss Guilford's cottage. "Couldn't afford that if I didn't knock up a fair bit: It's paid for," he added defiantly. "Aye! come on, let me take you for a ride on her."

His face was alive, his manner eager as he boasted of the speed it would do and the places he had been to faster than anybody else. "Come on," he coaxed her. "Just a little flip up Dark Lane and round back o' woods. If you like it we could go to Skeg or somewhere at the weekend."

Rachel shuddered. "Oh no thanks. I'm scared stiff of speed. Truly. I'd be petrified." Then a thought occurred to her. "Luke, if you are on nights, how are you able to go to the dance at the Welfare?"

The sulky look was back but he was only too willing to talk about himself.

"Well, like I said, I knock up a fair amount but I'm not workin' for th' government. Not me. They aren't having half my wages back in tax. When I've earned as much as I want for myself I go sick. See?"

Rachel frowned, unable to follow the logic of his argument.

"Don't worry, darlin'. Like I said, there's plenty. So will you come?"

"I'm sorry." Rachel shook her head. Her voice was gentle, her eyes begged him not to be hurt.

"But why? What else is there to do round here for God's sake?"

She hesitated on the brink of telling him she was writing a book. But he might want to know all about it and she did not know herself yet. So she fibbed a bit. "I'm researching. I can't tell you about it. It's private."

"Not every night you're not." He stared in huffy silence for a moment longer. "Oh well! Let me know if you change your mind but don't be surprised if I've changed mine." He had started to walk away and the last remarks were made with his back towards her, his head turned over his shoulder. "There's plenty round here would be only too glad of a night out wi' me. Don't you fret."

He sloped away towards his machine, straddled it, kicked the starter and revved the engine to a deafening pitch. He scootered his way over the bridge without another glance at Rachel. She cringed as he roared his way up through Upper Lynbury. When there was no sound of a crash she drew a deep breath and started for home.

"Noisy young devil." Mrs. Jakes was leaning over her garden gate. "He'll be getting himself into trouble one of these days. Himself, or somebody else." She squinted through her cigarette smoke at Rachel, who slowed down, smiled, said "Hello Mrs. Jakes," and quickened her pace again.

Mrs. Jakes looked after her, noting the proud, erect walk, the long slim legs. And the artists' brushes sticking out of her bag.

She shook her head slowly, brushed the

ash from the front of her dress and went indoors.

"Guess who I met in Nottingham?"

"Well whoever it was, put stars in your eyes."

Amy and Rachel were sitting in the garden drinking lemon tea. The red may, the laburnum and the lilacs were vying with one another in their splendour, while the sun, shining obliquely through the prunus, turned its unfolding leaves into wafer-thin laminae of mahogany.

"Who have you fallen in love with?" asked Amy.

Quick as light, Rachel slid out of danger. "I haven't fallen in love with anybody but there is a young man pestering me with his attentions." She told Amy about Luke's offer to take her dancing.

"Luke? Marilyn's boy friend? The one with the motor bike?" Amy looked anxiously at Rachel. "You will be careful love, won't you? I mean if he wants you to ride pillion or anything?"

"It's the *anything* you are worried about isn't it? Well don't. There's no need, honestly. I'm flattered but he's not my type." Rachel pressed the juice out of her lemon with a long spoon. "Young men are freaky. I prefer someone who's knocked about a bit and can talk of other things than motor bikes and dances."

Her eyes were dreamy. Amy watched her, then said quietly, "And so who did you meet in Nottingham?"

Rachel forced herself to meet Amy's gaze. And then she wished she hadn't. It was like sitting under a searchlight. "Oh, only Jonathan Blake." *Only!* What a worm she felt!

Grey eyes stared into brown while shadows dappled the grass and a cuckoo sounded not too far away.

"He's bought you a birthday present so I invited him round for a drink this evening. Is that all right?"

"Of course."

But Jonathan did not join them. He called with Amy's present while Rachel was showering. By the time she was dressed he had gone.

"He has an art dealer coming to see him," explained Amy. "He said it had slipped his mind when he accepted your invitation." There was a pause while Amy riffled through the pages of her birthday present. "You didn't tell me he had offered to take you with him into Derbyshire."

Rachel frowned, not liking the way Amy phrased that remark. It smacked too much of "giving the child a treat."

"I'm afraid I forgot," she said. "I was so angry with Luke for making a pass at me on the bridge, I forgot about poor old J.B."

Oh what treachery! She felt her tongue had twisted in her mouth like a corkscrew. The cuckoo called again and Rachel would not have been surprised to hear the cock crow thrice!

"Amy, if you don't want me to go, for any reason at all, you only have to say so. You wouldn't have to explain—"

Amy stared at her. "Mind? Why should I mind?" she asked coolly. She picked up her bag and gloves. "The only thing is, people might talk, it's so out of character. He usually likes to be alone."

She walked to the door unaware of the wild hope her words had aroused. Hope which was dashed to pieces in the next second.

"Of course, he did say he thought you were missing your parents. No doubt he sees himself as a father figure."

If Lena Sefton had said that, I would have called it sheer bitchiness, thought Rachel. But if Amy says he said it, then he said it.

But her optimism came to the rescue. Of course! He'd *have* to pretend to Amy. He might even be pretending to himself. Quite likely. Rachel smiled as they moved off in Amy's Mini.

It was nearly midnight. Rachel drew back the curtains and opened her bedroom window. The sky was full of stars and the night so quiet she could hear the water lapping over the stones.

By leaning out of the window, she could see the end of the bridge, but not the meadow or the studio. She contented herself by gazing in the general direction of it and tried to send her thoughts across the intervening cottages and trees.

Suddenly the peace was shattered by the sound of a car rattling down the main street towards the bridge. She saw the end of it more clearly as the headlight focused on it, then it was plunged into darkness again as the car turned the corner by the church. A door slammed and there was silence once more.

A breeze ruffled the curtains. Rachel shivered and got into bed.

6

THE following morning Rachel was splashing ineffectively but happily in the pool. Her eyes were closed, her face well clear of the water.

To her horror, for no apparent reason, the river came up and covered her. As she opened her mouth to scream, someone grabbed her ankles. Up went her legs and down went her head.

In the ageless seconds she was under the water, she was vaguely aware of the whiteness of that other pair of legs.

After what seemed an eternity she was held by the waist and set upright again. Retching and coughing, she fought to free herself of the encircling arm.

"Take it easy. You're quite safe." The laughter in the voice reassured but infuriated her. She squeezed the water from her face and found herself looking into the bluest eyes she had ever seen. And if that wasn't bad enough, they were topped by bright ginger hair.

"Yuk!" she said.

"Better now?"

"You slithy tove! You stupid oaf! How dare you come here and attack me like that? Who are you?"

"I'm Rupert," he said as though that explained everything.

Rachel glared at him, her eyes red from rubbing, her hair lank, the protective towel out of reach.

"Your shoulder strap's slipping," said Rupert. "Here, let me—" He reached towards her.

She tried to step back quickly and nearly slid under the water again.

"Whoops! Steady!" He grabbed her arm.

"Take your hands off me." She hitched up her strap and walked with as much dignity as she could muster, towards the steps.

Her face was sulky as she wrapped the towel around her shoulders and put on her sandals. Her chest ached from heaving and she felt humiliated. Having made up her mind, even before she met him, to dislike him, she resented the advantage he had over her. She started to walk towards the house.

"Aah! Don't go." He stood in front of her. His eyes were only a few inches above the level of her own. His face was thin and waif-like. So why should he have such a thick neck and sturdy shoulders, she wondered.

"Don't go," he repeated. "I'm sorry if I frightened you. Look, why not let me teach you to swim? I could you know. In half an hour from now you would never be afraid again of getting your head under water."

"No thanks. I don't care if I can't swim. I don't need to. I enjoy myself just flapping about. When I'm left alone," she added pointedly.

"But you might get into difficulty sometime."

"Not in water. I never go out of my depth so I'll never be in any danger." She answered without looking at him. Her tone was indifferent. She rubbed her arms with the towel.

"Suppose you fell off Lynbury Bridge. It's very dilapidated."

"The water is shallow there. Only a

small child could drown in it," she said loftily.

"You might fall overboard from a cross-channel steamer."

"If I can't afford to fly, I won't go." Rachel lifted a corner of the towel and wiped away the water trickling down her nose from her wet hair.

"What have you against being taught properly?"

"I'm unteachable. I have negative buoyancy. I was told so by the swimming instructor at school. I was allowed to cut swimming. I went for long walks instead."

"Negative what?" There were pin-points of light in the blue eyes. She eyed him suspiciously but his face was perfectly straight.

"Buoyancy." She rubbed her hair. "It's something to do with the disposition of weight and volume and specific gravity." Her voice was cool, off-hand, with the authority of someone who knew exactly what she was talking about. It was the only defence she had against the laughter in the blue eyes.

"Disposition of weight and volume— does that mean that although you have

100

everything, some of it is in the wrong place?" His eyes raked her from top to toe. "You could have fooled me."

"It means I shall never be able to swim. I go straight to the bottom," she said importantly.

The difference between her and the other girls at school had made her *feel* important. She looked at Rupert to see if he registered sympathy. After all, it could be dangerous.

"What a load of codswallop," said Rupert.

I was right, thought Rachel. I do loathe him. I shan't have to try. He's odious.

"Mum says I'm to take you home to breakfast." He had picked up his own towel and was zig-zagging it across his back.

"Tell your mother I thank her very much but Amy will have my breakfast ready by now."

"You'll be lucky. Amy's at our house tucking into kippers and fried tomatoes."

"What's she doing there?" Rachel stared at him, unable to believe such treachery. "What about me?"

Rupert was drying his legs. They were

white-skinned as a woman's but rock hard with muscle. As were his arms.

"She brought Mum a letter which the postman had left at your house by mistake. Mum invited her to stay and sent me to fetch you. Of course, if you don't want to join us you can go home and cook your own, unless you have some other disability which prevents you standing over a hot stove?" He looked her up and down again. "Negative buoyancy!" he jeered good-naturedly. "I've a good mind to chuck you back in the water."

Rachel backed away in alarm. "Don't you dare!" She was wiping her face, and the towel covered the lower half, leaving only her eyes exposed. They had lost their soreness and looked like great velvet discs. A mischievous light came into them. She lowered the towel and her expression was sweet.

"I am rather hungry," she said. "Will you wait while I go and get dressed? I won't be long." The smile she gave him was dazzling.

Rupert smiled, nodded, and turned away to pick up his trousers. As he bent down, Rachel moved swiftly, hand out-stretched—

But he had anticipated her mood. At the last moment he dodged aside. Carried forward by her own momentum, Rachel belly-flopped into the river again.

By the time she had finished spluttering he was dressed in trousers and tee-shirt and was sitting cross-legged on the grass watching her. He made no effort to help her.

"See what I mean? That could happen just as easily when you are by the Trent. You'd never get out of that."

"If I thought I'd ever be stupid enough to go near the Trent or anywhere else with you, I'd drown myself here and now." She stalked up the garden path, her sandals which had miraculously stayed on her feet, flapping wetly against her heels.

Rupert looked at the brightly coloured towel floating on the water like an exotic plant. He grinned, stripped down to his trunks again and went in after it.

During breakfast Rachel waited for Rupert to tell the others about the incident. He was sure to make fun of her.

She could imagine his gleeful chuckle, the quiet amusement of his mother and Amy.

But Rupert did not mention it. He was quietly attentive to the two older women, and his funny old-world courtesy, coupled with his gaiety, almost made Rachel wish she hadn't decided to dislike him.

"I heard that old banger of yours come limping down the lane last night," said Amy. "Why don't you get a new one?"

"It gets me where I want to go and it's never let me down yet."

"You've had it long enough and it wasn't new when you bought it. How old is it really?"

"Sixteen."

"Good heavens! Same age as Rachel." They all, including Rupert, particularly Rupert, looked at her.

She glared at them. "Why is everybody round here so obsessed with my age?" she asked grittily.

They stared at her in surprise. "What do you mean?" asked Amy.

"Oh nothing." She flushed, and humped her shoulders and was relieved when they started to talk to Rupert again.

Goodness! How easy it was to give yourself away!

Soon, Rupert excused himself saying he had some calls to make. Rachel couldn't understand the sudden pang inside her when he did not invite her to go with him.

"You're very quiet this morning," said Amy. "Are you feeling all right?"

"I'm fine. I swallowed a lot of water—"

"You actually got your face wet? Good gracious!"

Rachel looked suspiciously at the two women. Had they been watching from the end of Mrs. Kaye's garden? The amused, conspiratorial look was back.

"I'm afraid Rupert was rather frolicsome," she said loftily. "He's very young for his years. But then, boys are slow to mature aren't they?"

Amy and Mrs. Kaye looked at one another. Mrs. Kaye turned down the corners of her mouth comically, and laughed when she realised Rachel had seen the grimace.

"Mind you," Rachel said kindly, "I think he'll soon grow out of it. He's no worse than other boys of his age. It's just rather tiresome while it lasts that's all. All young boys are freaky."

Mrs. Kaye said, "I think you are in for a surprise Rachel." Her voice was mild but full of confidence. Amy said nothing. She was sitting with her elbows on the table, her head in her hands, but Rachel noticed the shaking of her shoulders.

Oh well, let them laugh, she thought. They'll soon find out I have a mind of my own.

"Thank you for a lovely meal," she said. "I'll do the dishes for you."

"Well I've met the wonderful Rupert and I'm not impressed," she told David Ramsey. "He's a mummy's boy."

Before David could answer, the bell jangled and Lena Sefton, cool and poised in cream linen, came in. Her bronze hair was burnished and full of life. She spoke to David, but ignored Rachel.

"David, could you copy this for me in time for the Garden Fete?" She held out a glossy magazine with the pages bent back to show a model leaning elegantly against a stone pillar.

They discussed materials and colours

and then David asked her if she wasn't going to speak to Rachel. "I know you two have met, so don't try to be funny, Lena." He pushed the magazine back into her hands. "Or you can go and get your frock made somewhere else."

Rachel waited for the explosion.

"Oh, is it Rachel?" Lena's voice implied she couldn't care less. "All young girls look alike these days. They have no individuality." She spoke as though she and David were alone in the room. But then she addressed Rachel directly.

"Your boy-friend's waiting for you on the bridge. Have you stood him up?"

She sounded amused, tolerant. The squire's wife making an effort to be nice to the cook's daughter.

For some reason she was not able to understand, Rachel immediately thought of Rupert. *Boy friend!* She flashed Lena a half scornful, half haughty look. But she didn't answer.

David grinned. "Who's this then, Rachel? Been unfaithful to me have you?" his grin said, "Don't let her rile you, ducky."

"I don't know what she's talking about," said Rachel.

"I'm talking about that handsome young man you were cuddling and kissing on the bridge the other day." Lena smiled her satisfaction when she saw the hot colour mount Rachel's cheeks. "J.B. and I were having a good laugh at the pair of you. 'Just look at them,' J.B. said. 'It makes me wish I were young again—'"

"I dare say it had a similar effect on you, too?" Rachel said sweetly.

Lena looked at her with a pretence of friendliness but her nostrils were dilating and her eyes glinted balefully.

"Poor little thing. I expect it's very lonely for you here. Very few boys of your own age. Of course, I know miners earn quite a lot of money these days but that young man has quite a reputation. However—"

Her smile, and the implication behind her words made Rachel feel shop soiled. She drew a deep breath and let it out slowly. There was an air of watchfulness about David and she could sense his sympathy towards herself, or rather his antipathy to Lena.

"Poor Luke," she said with an indulgent smile. "He wants to take me to the dance at the Miners' Welfare but unfortunately I'm going into Derbyshire with Jonathan and I don't know what time we'll be back." It's only a manipulation of the truth, she told herself. Not a real lie.

Lena's head jerked up and the angry colour seeped slowly over her cheeks and nose. (Her *long* nose, thought Rachel, comfortably) and down her face and neck.

Lena was still glaring when the bell jangled again. There was a scampering of feet on the stairs. Two little girls rushed into the room straight into David's outstretched arms.

"Uncle David—look what I've got."

David took the cheap plastic doll each child was holding out to him. Baffled, Lena stalked to the door.

"I'll come back when you're not so busy, David." As she went out, Mary Hornsby, the twins' mother came in.

Like her daughters, she had dark curly hair and blue-grey eyes. "Sorry if I came at the wrong moment David. But you know these two. Won't let me pass without coming in to see you." She smiled and her smile took in Rachel too. "Hello Rachel, lovely day isn't it? But what wouldn't I give for a shower of rain!"

Rachel got out the coffee cups while David swept the cutting table clear of material, shears and pins. He then picked up the children, one in each arm, and sat them on the table.

"Rachel, is Rupert home yet?"

"Yes. He came home last night." She remembered what Mrs. Kaye had told her about Mary and Rupert, and she smiled and added, "He sends his love."

David picked up some scraps of material and within minutes had transformed two cheap dolls into elegant models dressed in velvet and lace.

The children shrieked their pleasure and gratitude while Mary and Rachel chatted quietly together, exchanging information about themselves, tacitly agreeing they liked one another.

"David," said Rachel when they were alone together, "Would it be a good idea to take Mary out one night? Ask Rupert too—make it a foursome? It must be difficult for a young widow to have any social life—"

"A *splendid* idea ducky. She's having quite a job to adjust." He pushed at his fair hair, and twitched at the sleeve of his white embroidered shirt. "Tell you what —one of the Comedians is booked to come to the Welfare soon. I know she likes watching them on TV. There'll be dancing as well, after—"

"*If* we can get tickets. It's sure to be a popular night."

"Leave it to me. I'll get them."

Rachel, busy with needle and thread watched him covertly. David's hair shone, his skin was clear, his clothes immaculate. If only they weren't so outrageous!

"It was Mary who got me going in the rag trade," he said after a while. "I dressed her wedding. There were some big wigs from the colliery and their wives there, so it got a lot of publicity. Mary insisted that the papers printed 'Dresses designed by David Ramsey'. I've never looked back. And now," he said with one of his quick changes of direction. "What's all this about you going into Derbyshire with J.B.? Or did you just say it to annoy Lena?"

"No I'm going. But would you believe

111

it—he asked Amy's permission first. Amy says he believes I'm missing my daddy and he sees himself as a father-figure."

"That's a laugh. And I bet you anything you like Lena will find a way to stop you."

Rachel smiled serenely. "I think you underestimate Jonathan." She changed the subject quickly, not liking David's frown. "I haven't seen Henry for a long time. Is he ill?"

"Oh Henry doesn't socialise. Doesn't even come down to the pub any more. Drinks alone. He thinks people are laughing at him about Lena and J.B."

So I shall be doing Henry a favour if I can make Jonathan fall in love with me, thought Rachel. The idea was comforting. She bit off a length of thread.

"There you are David. Finished. Will you want me after lunch?"

"No thanks ducky. Go out and enjoy the sunshine. Give my regards to Rupert when you see him."

She scowled but did not answer.

There was a cold lunch waiting for her and a note from Amy. *"Had to rush off. Love. Ps. Rupert's coming for you at 3 p.m."*

Rachel ate her lunch and at two minutes to three she got out the ironing board and a pile of garments. At twenty past, she was still pressing a pair of slacks which already had a knife edge to them. He's not coming, she decided and put everything away.

She had just finished when he poked his head through the kitchen window. "Ready? Sorry if I kept you waiting."

"Ready for what?" she snapped. (I'm not angry with him for being late, she told herself. I'm angry that he's come at all.)

"I told Amy I'd be here at three but I was delayed—"

"I haven't seen Amy since breakfast time—"

"I thought she might have left a note."

Rachel was on the point of denying it when she caught his glance. He looked from her to the table where Amy's note lay.

"I'm busy. I've just ironed that lot." She pointed to the pile of garments.

"So. They won't want doing again will they?"

"No, but I'm going to wash my hair."

"Now? this very minute?"

"I ought to write to my parents." She felt herself weakening. He was charming though it nearly choked her to admit it. There was a courtesy behind his bantering manner. A gentleness which admitted a point of view other than his own, even while he queried it.

"Well if you won't come, I'll go and see my old flame." Rupert pushed himself back off the window sill.

"Your old flame? Who's that?"

"Lena Sefton."

"Pooh! I'm glad you said *old*."

"Some men prefer older women just as some women like older men."

She looked at him quickly. His expression held nothing but friendly amusement.

"When I was fourteen I thought she was the most beautiful girl I'd ever seen."

"And now?"

He looked at her gravely. "You are."

"I am what?"

"The most beautiful girl I've ever seen."

"I hate ficklety."

"There's no such thing. It's fickleness."

"Rubbish."

"What is?"

"Your conversation." She looked at him. "Go on then. Go and see Lena. But don't set her on fire with that awful hair."

"I'd rather go with you."

"I thought you'd never ask," she said, feeling as though she had scored off Lena. As she pulled the door to behind her she added, "But remember, I'm flameproof."

"Yes? But you aren't unsinkable."

"Slithy tove." It was nice, she thought, not having to put on an act. With Jonathan she tried to appear cool, sophisticated. His equal intellectually if not in years. With Luke she was on the defensive and felt guilty about it. He was as likeable as Rupert in his own way. So! If Rupert were a miner, Luke a lecturer in ornithology, and Jonathan a butcher.

A ripple of laughter shook her. As if life were not complicated enough!

"I don't suppose you'll be able to walk far on those spindly legs of yours—" Rupert was saying.

"You reckon?"

She lengthened her stride, swinging rhythmically from the hips. All the time she kept up a flow of small talk. She called

115

him a bird-watcher. He teased her about her "posh" accent.

They walked along Dark Lane and as they passed the studio they could hear the sound of angry voices, then Lena Sefton ran out. Rachel and Rupert slowed their pace in order to avoid confronting her for it was obvious she was in tears. Tears of rage judging by the way she stormed up the hill towards her home, thought Rachel.

"Ready for a rest?" asked Rupert as they followed the right of way behind the farm. The sun was hot, the sky blue, the path dusty.

"No, I'm used to walking." She hesitated, wondering whether to tell him about her Pennine walk. She was still smarting from the wound Jonathan had unwittingly inflicted. She coughed. "As a matter of fact, I walked the Pennine Way last year. With an organised party of course."

"You *what?*" Rupert stopped dead in his tracks and his look of incredulity was balm to her vanity.

"All two hundred and seventy miles—?"

"Every inch. Proper little masochist aren't I?"

Rupert's legs had got over the shock and were moving forward again. "Gosh! No! Don't say things like that. It's a marvellous achievement." He looked at her "spindly" legs and laughed. "I've often wanted to have a go, but honestly, I don't think I'd have the spunk."

"Oh you would." Rachel smiled, revelling in his admiration. And then she noticed something else. Rupert had the fine skin of red-haired people and the "V" left bare by his open-necked shirt was fiery. There was a red streak across his forehead too. She put a hand to her own head. "Fortunately the sun wasn't as hot as this or I'd never have made it. I'm afraid it's making my head ache. Silly isn't it?"

Rupert was full of concern. He led her into a small spinney and sat her down on a bed of last years leaves. She smiled and patted the ground next to her. They sat listening to the small sounds, the rustling of leaves, the twittering of birds and the bubbling of wood pigeons.

"Mary Hornsby was saying this morning she wished it would rain," said Rachel who could think of a no more interesting way of bringing Mary into the conversation. "She's a wonderful person. How she copes on her own I don't know. I expect she'll marry again in time. She's very attractive, don't you think so?"

"Hm mm!" Rupert's reply was a measure of his interest. Rachel decided to leave it for the time being. After all, she was supposed to have a headache.

After a while Rachel had the feeling she was being watched. There was a change of mood. Oh heavens! Don't say Rupert was going to make a pass at her. She opened her eyes briefly. He was leaning on one elbow, looking up at her.

"If I could remake your face I'd get rid of that idiotic little nose and substitute one with a bit of character."

"Like Lena Sefton's?"

"Your teeth are pretty. What have you got against Lena?"

"Nothing. I hardly know her. She thinks I'm after her boy-friend." She could have bitten off her tongue immediately she'd said it. Putting ideas into Rupert's head! She needn't have worried. He hooted with laughter.

"What—old J.B.? She must be mad. Do you know how old he is?"

"In his late forties I imagine. But what has age got to do with it?"

"A heck of a lot when it's coupled with other things like temperament, outlook on life, experience—that sort of thing. A blind man on a horse could see you're not his type."

"What do you mean by that? I'm a woman."

"Yes. But you're not a *man's* woman." He broke off as she sat up and glared at him.

"I beg your pardon?"

"I said you're not a *man's* woman. I mean —men like J.B. can look at a woman and know straight away whether she's likely to —if she'll—oh, you know what I mean."

He rolled over with his back to her. "Any man can tell. Not just him. I can tell."

"Tell what?" Rachel spoke softly but her eyes were angry.

"You know what I mean," he repeated. "You have a special look about you. Your sort are never found in the bargain basement. You are immaculate. Like

119

untrodden snow. A man like J.B. wouldn't give your sort a second thought."

The look of anger disappeared but was replaced by one of obstinacy. "There's a great deal of pleasure to be had from putting your foot in untrodden snow."

"Don't be silly Rachel."

The words inflamed her. "Don't talk to me as if I were one of your pupils." She stuffed a handful of dead leaves down his shirt neck then remembered the sore skin. "Sorry," she mumbled.

Rupert rolled over. "Wake me up when you're ready to go."

Rachel closed her eyes. I hate him, she thought. I'll show him whether I'm J.B.'s sort or not. But somehow a lot of the pleasure had gone out of the idea. A lot? Well, some of it. A bit.

She picked up a blade of grass, shredded it, threw it away and picked up a skeletal leaf. She held it by the stalk and twizzled it, wondering at the vague sense of disappointment. A sense of discontent which had nothing to do with what he had said about J.B.

"Rupert, have you ever been in love?"

"Frequently."

"Yes but seriously?"

"I'm always serious when I'm in love, aren't you?" The sense of disappointment deepened.

"I think we ought to be going."

He was on his feet instantly, offering her his hand. "How's the headache?"

"Better thank you." They were like polite strangers. He pulled her to her feet. He did not hold her hand a second longer than was necessary. They walked home with the sun behind them.

Later, when Amy learned how she had spent the afternoon and asked her if she had enjoyed it, Rachel said, "Well—you know. Rupert's nicer than I thought he was, in some ways, but he's awfully freaky. I expect he spends too much time with the birds. Feathered ones," she added at Amy's quizzical look.

Only then did she realise they had spent the whole time together talking about *her*. Not once had Rupert talked about his work. Thank heaven, she thought. All the same—

The telephone rang. Jonathan was going to Mill Dale in Derbyshire on Wednesday if it was fine. Would she like to come too.

Amy had given her permission. Rachel said, "Oh *yes!*"

And that's how long it took to wipe all thought of Rupert from her mind.

7

WEDNESDAY was a day of perfect happiness. A blue and gold day filled with the scents of summer, but because Amy had smelt rain in the air—never mind the weather men—Rachel wore coral coloured slacks and cotton shirt and carried a jazzy nylon mack.

Jonathan was in a terrific mood and monopolised the conversation except when they walked up-hill. They tramped across the soft, springy turf of Mill Dale, by the dew pond and the clump of beautiful trees, over a stile, and another one—"This will do," said Jonathan.

The valley fell away to the left and the scenery all around them was magnificent.

He showed her how to use a small cardboard frame to isolate one view from another and to relate what she saw in terms of a painted canvas, and she was delighted when he accepted her judgement.

She watched enraptured as he drew in the scene she had chosen. He worked quickly, for small clouds had begun to cast their shadow on the hillside. They were later than they had intended, for at the last moment, Lena who had promised to give them a lift to the bus station, had discovered she had a flat battery. Fortunately Henry had come back to the house to make a telephone call, and he had been delighted to come to their rescue with his Land-Rover. But the slight delay had made them miss their connection in Derby.

Rachel had to make quite an effort to squash the small feeling of triumph she had felt at Lena's plan coming unstuck. No doubt she would have her revenge, but Jonathan did not seem to be worrying, so why should I, she thought.

The picture was taking shape: dark greens and blues throwing into relief the softer colours of the valley. Rachel was surprised at the deep concentration necessary. Jonathan left all the talking to her now. She told him about her parents and their new marriages.

"They were very sensible about it," she

said. "Once they'd told me about it and found I wasn't upset, they just went ahead. They didn't wait for the divorce to come through. Mummy and Alex lived together and so did Daddy and Daphne. Much more sensible don't you think, than *pretending?* Anyway, Mummy said life was too short—"

She broke off. "Why have you painted the sky darker than the roof of the farmhouse?"

"Because it is darker."

He listened to her argument then proved to her she was wrong by making her look at the sky and the roof simultaneously through two small holes in a piece of card. She was amazed.

"Let that be a lesson to you," he said. "You know the roof *should* be darker than the sky so you saw what you expected to see. You forgot the sun. It's shining on the roof and making it almost white." He grinned at her. "The moral is—never take anything for granted, you may be deceiving yourself because of a preconceived idea."

Rachel wondered if there were more in that remark than seemed apparent to her at the moment, but she was too happy to care.

Darker clouds were building up in the distance and a soft, damp wind had arisen. Jonathan finished the broader washes of colour, and made detailed notes on the edge of the oiled paper he was using. He then made swift sketches of other parts of the valley.

"We'd better get down to the village," he said. "I can finish these in the studio. I won't have to bother about the changing light there."

Rachel would dearly have loved to ask him about Lena's ownership of the studio but decided it wouldn't do for him to know she had been gossiping about them. She remembered the angry voices she and Rupert had heard the other day, and Lena's rage as she ran from the studio.

But there was an air of confidence about Jonathan, an air of arrogance really. Was he so sure of her then? So sure she would not turn him out of his home?

They tracked down the valley to an inn where Jonathan ordered cold meat and pickles for them both, and a pint of beer for him and a shandy for Rachel. This delighted her. It was the first time she had been in a pub and the fact he had taken her there and ordered without reference to her age, made her think he had forgotten she was only sixteen.

They sat at a table near the bar and as they waited for their food to be served, a party of six—three men and three women —came in. While the men ordered drinks, the women glanced around the bar at the other customers.

One of them, a handsome, lusty, busty creature of about forty, fastened her gaze on Jonathan in a way which made Rachel blush for her. She looked quickly at Jonathan to see if he had noticed. He had. To her dismay he was gazing steadily, unblinkingly back at the woman.

It was not the impersonal gaze of an artist. It was a challenge recognised and accepted. Almost an embrace in itself. As if they were making love across the distance of the room. It reminded Rachel of the way Daddy and Daphne Compton had looked at one another in the early days of their friendship. Indeed, although she tried to push the thought away, it was a look she had often seen whenever a pretty woman had crossed his threshold.

Rachel sighed and shifted uncomfortably in her seat. Men were all alike, she decided. One just had to have patience.

The intimate look was broken by the arrival of the landlord's wife with their plates of beef. By this time the newcomers had been served and were moving down the bar to a table in the corner.

As they passed, the busty woman raised her glass to Jonathan. He smiled and lifted his tankard in acknowledgment. One of the other women, delicately juggling with handbag, cigarette and a glass of sherry, glanced at him and then at Rachel.

"My, my," she said. "Anybody would know you for father and daughter. Spitting image of you, she is."

Rachel looked frosty but Jonathan's eyes were twinkling at her across the table and one eyelid flicked down in a wink. She grinned and pulled a face which made him laugh out loud.

A veil of rain was obscuring the valley by the time they had finished their meal so they sat in cosy intimacy and talked. Jonathan talked. About art and artists. He told her about famous old masters who employed other artists to paint in the background of their pictures; of Hogarth who offended his sitters because he painted them exactly as he saw them, warts and all.

Rachel listened and laughed and watched as he lit another cigarette, surprised by the amount he smoked. He used a long holder and she noticed again how attractive his hands were, despite a few brown pigmentation marks on the backs of them.

They were big hands with long, bony fingers and perfect nails which extended a little way beyond his finger tips and were filed to a perfect oval.

She thought of Luke's capable hands and his filbert nails rimmed with dirt. Unlike Luke, Jonathan was aware of the attractiveness of his hands and used them a lot when he talked.

Rachel was not looking at him directly but was watching his reflection in a mirror. His movements were co-ordinated like the movements of a trained actor. He had an actor's presence too, and a manner of projecting his personality. He was speaking softly yet most people in the bar were looking at him with interest. Men as well as women. As though they were wondering if he were somebody important.

Not surprising really, thought Rachel. He was wearing a dark red open-necked shirt, perfect with his bright pewter-coloured hair, the brown skin and the flashing dark eyes. His appearance was devastating. You couldn't blame people for staring. She felt an uprush of love and pride.

He was telling her now about the camera obscura which many of the old masters had used.

She sighed. "Oh what a lot of interesting things I don't know. I feel as if I have wasted my life."

Just then there was a great shout of laughter from the six people at the other table. Someone had told a joke, someone else was trying to cap it. They were the centre of attention now. The man and the young girl were forgotten. They looked at one another and smiled. And then it happened.

Jonathan took Rachel's chin in his hand

and stared into her eyes for several seconds while she gazed solemnly back at him.

"Your life is only just beginning my dear. Don't waste it chasing shadows."

And then he kissed her. His lips barely brushed her cheek while at the same time his hand rumpled her hair. An avuncular gesture.

But Rachel clung to him, entirely unprepared for the thrill which set her whole body shaking. He pushed her away quickly but she knew that the truth had shone out from her eyes. The truth of her love for him.

He looked at her for a startled moment longer then he gently chucked her under the chin with his clenched fist.

"You are a grand kid, Rachel. I don't know what the young men are thinking of, to stand idly by while you take an old man out for the day."

Rachel's heart was pounding, her lips trembling, her eyes held a suspicion of tears. Her voice, when she found it, was only slightly husky.

"Young men? Pooh! They're freaky."

All the way home her heart was singing because she knew, she *knew* now that he loved her. "He loves me, he loves me. He doesn't want to because he thinks I'm too young, but he *does* and I will make him admit it before long."

"I will. I *will*." And then she frowned because there was so little time.

For the next few days Rachel moved as though in a dream. Her thoughts of Jonathan coloured her whole existence. Out walking the country lanes with Rupert, sewing buttons and pressing frocks for David, helping Amy about the house, shopping—all these duties were performed in a state of euphoria which lasted until it dawned on her that Jonathan was deliberately avoiding her and that far from seeking to revenge herself, Lena seemed closer to him than ever.

After a while, Rachel had convinced herself that Jonathan was fighting his love for her and was deliberately allowing Lena to dominate him.

The portrait of Lena was finished and yet, thought Rachel, she spends more time than ever at the studio.

Mrs. Jakes confirmed this. With her

cigarette wagging about on her bottom lip and her eyes screwed up, she held forth.

"There'll be trouble up there before long. You mark my words. She leaves home in that car of hers as though she's going to Nottingham or somewhere and she gets no farther than the studio. She must think her husband's daft. He's only got to go in the top meadow and he can see that yellow sports car as plain as plain. And he knows the portrait's finished. Urr well! It's no skin off my nose."

Mrs. Jakes was pretending to talk to David but Rachel knew the remarks were directed at her. Odious woman! She watched the hot ash fall. I wish David would stop her coming here before we all go up in flames.

And so Rachel sulked and fretted in a fever of impatience because the time was drawing near for the honeymooners to return, and fresh plans would be made for her.

And then one day, one dreadfully humiliating day—She had seen Jonathan getting on the bus in Upper Lynbury. On her way home across the footbridge, she had felt an unconquerable longing to go to

133

the studio, just to be near the place where he lived. Why not? What harm could there be in just walking casually along Dark Lane, and knocking on his door as though she had a message for him from Amy? No harm at all, she decided, making sure there was no yellow car outside.

Walking alongside the meadow between the bridge and the studio she saw Marilyn lolling on the grass. Surprisingly, she was alone. Rachel remembered it was early closing day at the greengrocers where Marilyn worked and she supposed that Luke, her bold-eyed boy-friend was sleeping before going on night shift at the pit.

She waved as Marilyn looked up but the girl made no sign of recognition. Yet she watched Rachel all the way and at last got up and followed her.

Rachel went up the path to the white door and lifted her hand to the knocker. And then she saw the key was in the lock.

Her first reaction was surprise that Jonathan could be so careless in view of Henry Sefton's jealousy. Suppose Henry came down and damaged Lena's portrait?

Or vandals? Think of the damage they could do with oil paint and turpentine!

Should she lock the door and take the key home with her, and so give herself a genuine excuse to see him again? She could leave a note telling him what she had done.

She searched her bag, tore a leaf out of her diary but could find neither a pencil nor a ball-pen. She stood for a moment, wondering—

It wouldn't hurt, would it? Just to go inside and see if she could find anything to write with? Just a little peep?

She pushed the door gently—put her foot over the threshold.

"What the devil do you think you're doing!"

Rachel spun round at the sound of the hard, metallic voice. The key dropped to the ground.

They stood staring at one another, the slim, dark eyed girl and the predatory tiger.

Lena's tawny eyes were wide with anger but she was in perfect control of herself.

Not so Rachel. The colour which had left her face at the sound of Lena's voice came flooding back. She looked a picture of guilt and incompetence.

"I was—I mean—I thought—" she stammered incoherently.

Lena's anger turned to contempt. She held out her hand. "My key. *If* you don't mind."

Miserably, Rachel picked up the key and put it in the outstretched hand. Lena did not speak again but her eyes flashed the message. "Get out!"

Rachel, dumb with shock and humiliation, crept away.

Marilyn's voice was full of mock sympathy as Rachel passed her. "Aah! Bad luck!" her raucous laugh echoed all along the river bank.

The memory tortured Rachel for days. Why hadn't she stood up to Lena? Why had she let herself be treated like a naughty schoolgirl? In front of Marilyn too! It was stupid. All she'd had to do was say she thought Jonathan was in. Lena didn't know she'd seen him getting on the bus. But though she blamed herself for losing her presence of mind, most of her anger was for Lena.

Coupled with this was the deadness

round her heart because Jonathan was still avoiding her. And because Lena had her own key!

She saw him one day, coming out of the barber's. He nodded, turned, and walked quickly away in the other direction. On one miserable occasion she met him at the Rectory in company with other people who had been invited to discuss the plans for the Garden Fete. She was desolate when he treated her with casual courtesy and then ignored her altogether. She could not understand it. They had been so happy that day in Mill Dale. Her feeling for him was so strong she could not, *would* not believe he was not affected too. He *must* feel something for her.

She admitted to herself that at first, it had been a game, this determination to make him love her, then it had become a longing. Now it was an obsession.

Without thinking of the actual mechanics of sex, she wanted him to love her as she had never wanted anything before. She wasn't fooling herself, was she? She remembered the way he had looked at her in the pub. The kiss. The fact that she was the only person he had ever invited out on a sketching trip—

She played the childish game of "if I can count up to a hundred before the sun goes behind a cloud, I shall know he loves me." And she would count very quickly.

Adolescents do nothing by halves and Rachel was no exception. Her appetite deserted her; her eyes became dull and strained through loss of sleep. She began to feel dissociated from the real things of life. He possessed her thoughts every hour of every day until she was nothing but a web of childish feelings, ready to burst into tears at the slightest provocation.

If Amy worried about the change in her, she kept her thoughts to herself. When Rupert looked bewildered by Rachel's moods Amy spoke to him with her lips, not her voice. "Growing pains," she said. Rupert nodded and stayed away for several days.

And then the letter came from Yugoslavia. It was from Daddy to say Mummy had fallen down some steps and was in hospital with a broken leg. She was being very well treated and was quite happy and not at all upset that she and Alek would have to stay on for a few more weeks.

"She will be writing to you herself in a day or two. Daphne and I are coming home next week and are going to live in Norfolk as arranged. You can either join us or wait for Mummy and Alek to come home. I expect you'd like to stay with Amy a little longer wouldn't you?"

Knowing Daddy, bless him, the message was clear. Stay put.

Amy was willing but she said quietly, "You know I never pry, but if someone is upsetting you here, wouldn't it be better to leave? Sometimes, running away is the best, the *only* thing to do."

Rachel smiled wanly and shook her head. It was unthinkable. She put her arms round Amy and rested her cheek against her shoulder. "Sorry if I worried you. Please let me stay, I'll be all right now. And thank you for not asking questions."

She sighed and straightened her shoulders. "I suppose I've been upset at the thought of leaving you and Rupert."

She smiled and looked Amy straight in the eye. "*Dear* Rupert. I've missed him so much but I couldn't very well tell him what was worrying me, could I?"

Amy's expression was inscrutable. "Of course not love."

Minute by minute Rachel became more cheerful. "I'd like to send Mummy some flowers through Interflora. I expect it will cost the earth but Daddy's sent me another cheque. What do you think?" She looked appealingly at Amy.

"Of course love. Help me clear up then go and see about it."

"And then I'll go and see Rupert. I *have* missed him." In Rachel's mind the "him" meant Jonathan.

Amy smiled. "You do that," she said.

And so was perpetuated once more, one of the delusions of the young, that brash, hurriedly constructed lies, fool some of the people all of the time.

8

RACHEL looked up to find Rupert leaning on one elbow, looking down on her as she lay on the grass. He laughed triumphantly.

"I willed you to open your eyes."

Rachel sat up. "You did nothing of the kind. I opened them because I wanted to."

He shook his head. "I looked at you and willed you. That's why you wanted to."

"Are you suggesting you have the power to make me do things I don't want to do?"

He lay back and put his arms under his head. "No. But it's easy to make people do consciously the things they want to do *sub*consciously."

"Meaning that although I was enjoying a nap in the sun, what I really wanted to do was sit and gaze at you? Red hair an' all?"

She was indignant because it was so near the truth. She had been lying there with her eyes closed, sensing Rupert's gaze on her—wondering if he were trying to pluck up the courage to kiss her—wondering if she would be pleased or sorry if he did.

She was not in love with him but was young enough to enjoy the idea of him falling in love with her. It made her feel important; made Rupert more interesting to her; added excitement to her life.

There was no awkwardness in her relationship with him. Their ease in each other's company sprang not so much from sex as from the need of youth for youth.

Occasionally she found herself wondering if he had had much experience with women. He was courteous in all his dealings with her. A kind, considerate friend who made no attempt to attract her.

Sometimes, conscious of his gaze, she would look at him, enquiry in her eyes. He would smile serenely but there was that in his expression which made her feel humble, yet when next he spoke it would be of unimportant things. His silences were far more eloquent than anything he said.

In order to give substance to the lie she had told Amy two weeks ago about her feelings for Rupert and her dismay at having to leave him, she had spent as much time with him as possible, pushing her thoughts of Jonathan as far into the background of her mind as they would go. She had decided to let things take a natural course but to be on the look out for any opportunity to get back on a friendly footing with him.

Meanwhile, she and Rupert were constant companions. They played tennis, foursomes, at Rachel's suggestion with Mary Hornsby and David Ramsey. David was an indifferent player and as Rachel had anticipated, he would soon drop out of a game, then he and Rachel would sit on the park bench and watch Mary and Rupert battle it out.

Sometimes the four of them would have a boat out on the lake in the grounds of Nottingham University or they would walk across the fields to Newstead Abbey, now a ruin but once the home of the Byron family. They would admire the gardens and the lake, and read the poem on the monument which Lord Byron had erected to the memory of his dog, Bosun.

Always on these outings, Rachel contrived to pair off with David, leaving Mary and Rupert together. It delighted her to see how well they got on. Mary was knowledgeable about the countryside and knew the names and calls of most wild birds. Rupert talked to her about his work as he had never talked to Rachel.

And then David began excusing himself owing to pressure of work. The autumn and winter orders were coming in. Mary stayed away too. The twins had been on a visit to their Granny's. Now they were back.

Rachel still helped David in the mornings but her afternoons and evenings were free. She and Rupert continued to see a lot of one another.

One of their favourite spots was the top of the hill behind the Seftons' farm. They would sit and look at the village spread out below them, the church, the old cottages, the woods and pastures. They could see the hens scratching in Mrs. Jakes's garden at the end of Dark Lane; and the yellow car outside Jonathan Blake's studio. They often saw Marilyn in the meadow, sometimes alone, often with Luke.

Sometimes they sat until the sun went down and shadows crept over the landscape, giving back to the flowerbeds in the gardens below them, the colours they had temporarily lost in the bright sunlight.

They walked up the hill one night in bright moonlight when the air was full of subtle scent not noticeable in the daytime.

Even the pit-head stocks took on a gaunt beauty at these times and Rachel's heart was sad because Rupert was beside her and she ached for Jonathan.

But her respect for Rupert was growing. He was no man's fool despite his gentleness. And whereas Jonathan talked to her, fed her information with the ease and fluency of a professional lecturer, Rupert, who was one, didn't, she thought ruefully. He argued with her, made her explain her judgements.

She knew as soon as she saw and heard Henry Sefton with his shot-gun letting fly at the pigeons which were marauding his crops, that she would say the wrong thing. But she tried to say the right one.

"What a pity in these days of scientific miracles that somebody can't find a painless way of keeping down the number of pests. Some of those birds might only be injured. They could take hours to die."

Rupert was watching Henry. "I'm glad he saw us come up here. I wouldn't like him to point that gun this way." Suddenly Henry turned and waved as though to reassure him. Rupert sighed his relief and turned to Rachel.

"Why do you think it necessary to keep down the number of pests as you call them?"

"Well they *are* pests. Pigeons and rabbits. They do untold damage to farm crops and there *is* a world food shortage."

"Granted. But why blame the pigeons and rabbits? Why not blame humans for over-breeding?"

"You think the human race should be culled?"

Rupert laughed and tickled her nose with a piece of grass. "Not quite. But humans do have the intelligence and the means to regulate their numbers so why should they be allowed to increase at the expense of wildlife? Hm?" He smiled and waited but she did not know the answer.

"Everything is put into this world for a purpose. Nature is quite capable of taking care of itself. Instead of saying there are too many rabbits, give them myxamatosis

—too many foxes, set the dogs on them, too many seals, skin them alive, we should be saying, there are too many humans, let's do something about it before it's too late."

He waited for her to argue. After a lot of thought she said, "That doesn't apply to Britain though. Only to overcrowded countries like China and India. And even there—I was reading in the colour supplements—they are being encouraged to practise birth-control."

Rupert sat up and linked his arms round his knees. "But why do you think population control is more important there than here?"

Another long silence. "Well. Obviously. The people are poor. Primitive conditions. Overcrowding." She was thinking of the pictures she had seen. Old people with hardly any flesh on their bones; thin, half-starved children with empty rice-bowls.

"Think of one child born under those conditions and one born in a highly civilised country. Which child will be the bigger drain on the world's natural resources? And don't forget, Britain has a greater density per square mile than either China or India."

"It *has?*" That really surprised her. But then, Rupert was always surprising her. Irritating her too, because she could not challenge his statements. For all she knew, he could be miles out.

All the same, she remembered most of the things he told her and the next time she was with Jonathan she would have lots of talking points. She would say, "I was reading the other day that—" and they would be off.

Not that Jonathan was concerned about conservation. Or population explosion. So long as it didn't explode on his favourite bits of Derbyshire, he would never notice.

She closed her eyes and imagined herself polishing up her newly acquired bits of information and dazzling him with her conversation. She would gently lead up to the fact that in her opinion it was a crime to have more than one child per family. She wouldn't dream of having any at all.

And that was another thing. She looked at Rupert. "With your views," she said quietly, "you will have to go through life childless. Unless you intend marrying a widow with a ready-made family."

The silence was longer than any that had gone before.

"If it's Mary Hornsby you are thinking about, forget it."

Rachel leapt to Mary's defence. "Why? She's young. Pretty. You have a lot in common. And you don't argue with her like you do with me."

She looked at him and waited. This could be his cue if it was herself he wanted. He didn't speak, so, slightly ruffled, she went on, "I know it's too soon yet, but—"

"Soon or late, it makes no difference. Are you blind? Don't you know David is head over heels in love with her? When he goes away, Mary and the twins will go with him—"

"David? *David Ramsey?* You must be mad!"

"Oh? Why do you say that?" Rupert was using a blade of grass to transfer a beetle from his trousers to Rachel's bare leg.

She flicked it off, trying to remember something David had said. "I was always different. It must have been the result of her (his mother's) deep longing for a daughter. Didn't quite make it poor old love." She had assumed—she coloured hotly. Well who wouldn't? His smooth skin, his silky hair, the frilly shirts and exotic suits he wore—

"Don't get David wrong," said Rupert. "Lots of men, most of us, have a feminine streak, just as most women have a masculine one. David, for business reasons, exaggerated his." He grinned at Rachel. "Can you imagine what life would have been like for him in Lynbury if he hadn't masqueraded as a—well—as a man who wasn't interested in women? They would have eaten him alive. He's too vulnerable. There was a woman once—tried to inveigle him into something. When she failed she made accusations. Her husband, a miner, went to see David, breathing fire and brimstone. Took one look at him and burst out laughing. Took his wife home and gave her the hiding she had hoped he would give David. That clued David up."

Rupert grinned at Rachel's red face. He brought his hand down heavily on her knee and leaned on her.

150

"Let that be a lesson to you. Never judge by appearances."

She brushed his hand away. Never judge by appearances. You may be deceiving yourself because of a preconceived idea. That's what Jonathan had said to her that day in Derbyshire. Just another way of telling her she couldn't see further than the end of her nose. And she couldn't. Fancy not noticing about David and Mary! Trouble was, she was so full of her own selfish motives—hello! Rupert was watching her intently. What now? Don't say he was working himself up to a proposal! Urr well! as Mrs. Jakes would say.

"Rachel—"

"Hm?"

"May I ask you something?"

"Hm mmm."

"Why did you go out with J.B. for the day? What can you possibly have in common with a man like him?"

Rachel sat up straight. There was an eyeball to eyeball confrontation. Brown and blue. And the brown were mutinous.

"Rupert dear, that is none of your business."

"It is my business. I'm fond of you and I don't want you to get hurt."

"Ha! People always say that when they disapprove of what I do. Nobody worries about me being hurt when I'm doing what *they* want me to."

"That's not true. Don't you care if people talk about you? Nastily, I mean?"

"No." Her eyes were cold. Cold as a November day.

He studied her for a long time. "You little fool."

"Get lost Rupert." She turned away.

"You aren't falling for him are you?"

There was so much gentle anxiety in his voice that Rachel's anger evaporated, even though she could not be sure whether his anxiety was for her or himself.

"I did have a bit of a crush on him when I first met him," she said. And she laughed, hoping by her laughter to persuade him that what she said was not true.

"Come off it. A lovely girl like you?" Rupert's hand lay on the grass between them. A white hand with pink, knobbly knuckles, short nails and a half healed cut on one of his fingers. "Did you—I mean did he—try to kiss you or anything?"

Rachel sat very still, resenting Rupert's question, denying his right to ask it. But because of a mind made sensitive by her feeling for Jonathan, she wanted to show him compassion; wanted to beg him not to become too fond of her, to stop thinking of her in those terms before he too, got hurt.

It was a mistake, she realised now, to have spent so much time with him, raising his hopes—

There was a movement beside her. She had not answered his question, and by the look on his face he had drawn his own conclusion. He was standing over her, pulling her to her feet.

"Time to move. It's getting chilly." It was too. The sun had dipped behind the trees and their side of the hill was in the shade. But some of the chill was in Rachel's own heart. She frowned and wondered why. Why should it bother her that Rupert was refusing to look at her and that his manner was distant?

She felt a sudden rush of anger. It wasn't as though he had admitted being in love with her himself. All he had said was that he was *fond* of her.

Rupert still had hold of both her hands and for one moment as they faced one another, she lifted her face and swayed her body towards his, pressing hard against him.

He looked at her, his face tense. He tightened his grip on her hands, holding her away from him, then he let her go, and turned away.

They walked side by side down the hill in silence. Rachel couldn't tell what he was thinking, but for herself, she was full of loathing.

Why had she tried to tease him like that? So that she could have the satisfaction of refusing him? *No. No.* Why then? Mercilessly she kept asking herself why? Finding no answer, her thoughts turned to Rupert. What had he thought? Had she cheapened herself in his eyes? Selfishly, all the way home she wondered what *he* had thought of her. What had made her do such a thing.

It never occurred to her that Rupert might be blaming himself. That he might be thinking he had pulled her off-balance.

That he too might be feeling self-disgust and was in need of reassurance.

They did not meet again until the night they went to the Miners' Welfare with David and Mary. There was a cool breeze and a slight drizzle so they went by the main road in Rupert's "banger".

After the guest star, a well known comedian had entertained the customers, there was dancing until midnight. The small steel band was good and noisy. The main lights were turned off and piercing streaks of red and blue and green lights played on the dancers. There was an excellent bar and the four of them were relaxed and happy. They danced a lot in twosomes, foursomes, groups and lines. Whatever was going they were part of it. There was no sign of tension between Rupert and Rachel now, and when they were not dancing he and David kept the girls in fits of laughter. David was a brilliant, wicked mimic. He took off Rachel's posh accent, Lena Sefton's metallic drawl, Mrs. Jakes's "Urr well!" Then he changed his voice and became a wriggling, writhing pop singer.

Towards midnight Marilyn passed their table with three youths and another girl. She looked haughtily at Rachel and her friends but didn't speak.

"Hello," called Rachel, cheerfully. "Where's Luke?"

Marilyn paused. "If you *must* know, he's at work tonight." Her voice and manner were pert because it was Rachel who asked the question. But it was Rupert she was looking at.

One of the boys pulled roughly at her arm. "Come *on*," he said. And Rachel recognised him and his pals as the three youths who were lolling about outside the Welfare the first time she had met Luke.

"Roughnecks," she murmured as they slouched away. Nobody spoke. She caught a significant movement of Mary's eyes and smothered a laugh as she saw that both Rupert and David were fascinated by the sight of Marilyn's plump little bottom wriggling away in its tight skirt.

"Oy!" Rachel said, passing her hand in front of Rupert's eyes.

They all laughed, then, "Who's for fish and chips?" asked David. "Let's get some and eat them in the car."

"Why do they taste so much better out of a bag?" Mary asked later as they sat munching.

"And why does coffee always smell better than it tastes?" asked Rachel.

"Only when you make it ducky," said David.

The two girls were in the back seat. David and Rupert half turned towards them. Rachel saw the gang first.

"Trouble," she said.

People were drifting out of the Welfare and walking away. But the three youths with Marilyn and her friend had been joined by another one and they were all heading towards the car.

The four youths made a rush, took hold of the front bumper and bounced the car up and down.

David's window was down in a flash. "Cut it out, you lot. Unless you want me to come and sort you out."

There was a yell of laughter from the gang. One of them minced up to the open window and leaned towards David.

"Oh I say, Mavis," he lisped prettily. Then he pursed his lips and made a kissing noise. "How's the frock trade darling?

157

Will you make me a frilly nightie—?"
There was another burst of laughter and
more jeers. Marilyn and the other girl were
shouting, "Bounce 'em lads. Bounce 'em."

"Rupert, let's go. I'm frightened," said
Mary.

Rupert finished his chips, screwed up
the bag, dropped it in the waste bin and
switched on the ignition. The youths
grabbed the bumper again and lifted it.

Without a word being spoken, Rupert
got out one side, David the other.

Marilyn and her girl-friend backed
away. The youths were defiant, aggressive.
There was a scuffle during which David
changed from an elegant couturier into a
lithe, hard-to-hit young man with a
workman-like left hook which must have
made his Great Uncle Alfred squirm
delightedly in his grave.

One of the youths went reeling back-
wards, landed at Marilyn's feet and stayed
there.

Rachel's hand flew to her mouth when
a moment later, she saw Rupert take a
nasty blow to the head, then she smiled as
he slowly and systematically took the
youth apart. He finally demolished him

with a few short jabs to the ribs and a cracking blow to the jaw.

"Oh well hit sir!" she cried. Then she gasped as she saw a third youth aim a kick at David's groin. David was quick. A grab at the ankle, a jerk and the youth was flat on his back. David lifted him by the hair, let him go and sent him down again with a blow so fast Rachel hardly saw him move.

"Three down one to go," she chirruped. And laughed as the last of the gang turned and ran. "Three cheers for Great Uncle Alfred."

They watched Rupert mopping a cut on his face. David, less elegant than Rachel had ever seen him, walked over to the two youths who were lolling on the pavement near Marilyn and the other girl. At his approach the girls giggled and moved away. Marilyn sidled up to Rupert.

Rachel wound her window down in time to hear her say, "Good old copper-knob. You wouldn't like to give me a lift home would you dearie?"

"You'd better take your boy-friends home. They aren't fit to be out alone," said Rupert. He grinned at her. Marilyn seemed reluctant to move.

159

And then Rachel heard something which made her open her eyes wide and cover her ears with her hands. David was telling the youths what they could expect if they ever annoyed him or his friends again.

"What *language!*" she whispered to Mary. "Great Uncle Alfred again?"

Mary nodded, too overcome with laughter to speak.

The youths slunk off in one direction, the girls in another. Rachel watched as Marilyn, tossing her lovely blonde hair over her shoulder, turned, called out something to Rupert and made a kissing noise.

"Be seeing you dearie," she called.

David and Rupert got into the car, grinning sheepishly. Mary reached over and brushed her hand over David's shoulder. It was like a caress. Rachel wore a smile which threatened to split her face in two.

"Good old copper-knob," she mimicked. "Like to see me home dearie?" Then apropos nothing but her own happy thoughts she began to sing. *"There were three in a bed and the little one said, Roll over, roll over. They all rolled over and one fell out. There were two in a bed—"*

It was ridiculous and not even relevant. She was off-key, slightly tom-cattish—

Suddenly they were all doubled up with laughter. Even the old car seemed to have caught the mood for instead of moving round a curve in the road, it went straight on into the ditch—

They were still laughing when the Panda car drew up in front of them.

"Good evening sir. Had a good time?"

"Absolutely splendid officer." A trickle of blood ran down Rupert's face. His hair stood on end like a fiery halo. "This is a nasty bend. I don't suppose you'd give us a hand with the car, would you?"

"First things first sir. Would you mind blowing into this little bag—?"

Rachel pushed open her bedroom window and looked in the direction of the studio. It was the first time she had thought about Jonathan for almost four hours. She looked up at the stars, listened to the sound of the river. A nightbird called.

She sighed happily and got into bed.

9

"THANK you Rachel dear. So kind of you. Do come in and have a cup of tea with us."

US? Rachel had been shopping for Miss Guilford. Now, heart beating in anticipation, she followed the old lady into her sitting-room.

And there he was, silhouetted against the sunlit window. His big frame almost blocking out the light. Jonathan Blake smiled. "Hello Rachel."

A great shiver went through her body. Her heart lurched and then seemed to stop. She felt herself grow pale. The dark enchantment was still at work.

With a tremendous effort she steadied herself, smiled, and said, "Oh hello Jonathan." And turned her attention to Miss Guilford.

They sipped their tea, ate homemade cake and chuckled over Rachel's account of the evening at the Welfare and the punch-up afterwards. Rachel asked him briefly about Lena's portrait, then started to talk to Miss Guilford about her garden.

Although she made light of it, the old lady's arthritis was troubling her so Rachel washed the tea things and promised to call again the next day to see if there was anything she could do to help her. Her bright smile as she left, included Jonathan.

After that, hardly a day passed without Rachel calling in on Miss Guilford. Sometimes she would help with household chores which arthritic hands found difficult. On sunny days she would inspect the garden for chickweed and mares' tails and when she'd pulled them out she would carry them to the compost heap in the corner and would linger there, for that part of the garden was nearest to the studio. Sometimes she would just sit and talk to Miss Guilford and listen to her stories of Lambarene. If Miss Guilford noticed on these occasions that Rachel always placed herself near the big bow window which overlooked the garden, the river and the studio, she made no comment. Sometimes, Jonathan had tea with them and when he did, Rachel treated him casually and talked a lot about

Rupert. And she was happy to notice the silvery head was turned often in her direction, and the dark bird-like eyes were friendly.

One day when the three of them sat under the transluscent shade of the apple tree, he asked Rachel if she would like to see his studio. Her heart lurched but when she answered her manner was off-hand.

"Some other time, perhaps. It's so lovely sitting here." She managed an ordinary, friendly smile and prayed he would try to persuade her to change her mind.

In the event it was Miss Guilford who did that. "I shall be going out in a little while Rachel. Stay here as long as you like of course, but—"

Bless you. Oh *bless you*. Rachel stretched gracefully as a cat and smiled at Jonathan. "In that case I'd love to come."

The studio surprised her. She had expected masculine disarray and the smell of turps. What she had not expected was the harmonious effect that had been created by odds and ends of furniture, none of which had individual merit.

The wicker-chair, the marble-topped wash-stand; the old piano littered with dog-eared music. The divan pushed against the wall in the corner under the bookshelves had a Spanish style cover in shades of blue and green. Curtains and cushions were peacock blue against white brick walls. Rush mats littered the floor. Rachel flipped through the music.

"I see you and Amy have the same taste in music as well as tea-shops," she said.

He didn't answer and she moved away to a stack of paintings at the working end of the studio. "All landscapes of Derbyshire," she said inspecting them.

"Come over here and tell me what you think of this." Jonathan had pulled back a curtain which concealed an alcove. Rachel gasped. Lena Sefton! There she was in all her tawny beauty. The magnificent hair, the long nose, the parted but unsmiling lips. And that skin! The portrait was so life-like Rachel almost expected to see Lena step from the canvas and make her insolent, hip-swinging way across the room.

"Isn't she superb?" It was a statement not a question. And the way he said it brought tears to Rachel's eyes. Somehow, the portrait made her feel small, insignificant and depressed. All the bright colours of the day faded for her.

It was terrible to be forced to the realisation that they had spent hours cooped up together with her like *that*. Stark naked. It was unbearable. She hadn't thought—

"I suppose you've painted lots of women like that? In the nude?" Her voice was doleful.

"Dozens. Are you shocked?"

"Good heavens, no," she said stoutly. "I was just thinking how difficult it must be holding a pose like that for hours on end." Quietly fishing.

"Not difficult. Impossible. We work for an hour then rest. Mrs. Sefton is a fantastic model. She's able to drop straight into position every time and to hold it without wilting."

Rachel felt a surge of envy. "It must be marvellous to be a model. I wish—" She turned and looked at him.

He closed the curtain. "Nothing doing little Rachel."

"I meant with my clothes on," she said brightly as though she were joking.

A laugh spurted from him. "I certainly wouldn't paint you with them off—"

"Oh wouldn't you?" Again her voice was cheerful. As though they were discussing whether or not they would walk in the garden in the rain. "Why not?"

"You'd be in tears in ten minutes. It's a terrible ordeal for a novice. Especially a girl like you."

"Aah! End of me as a model. Oh well!" She turned to face him, her eyes full of laughter. Willing him to see her as a woman to be reckoned with instead of a teenage girl.

He moved back to the alcove, drew the curtain and moved the portrait to one side.

"Come over here," he said. "Sit down, make yourself comfortable and relax."

Alive with excitement she slipped off her shoes and stepped on to the small dais. While he selected paper and charcoal she experimented with various positions, finally settling for one she fondly imagined was the same as the one Lena held. One leg straight out, one knee bent upwards, weight on the top half of the body supported by backward stretching arms. She let her head droop back slightly. She parted her lips but did not smile.

Jonathan did. "Sit up properly there's a good girl."

Nursery talk. But she sat up without a word.

"That's better." The impersonal expression was back. "Put your head a little to the left—tuck in your chin."

She tried to do as he asked but her limbs felt stiff and awkward. She felt like one of the little wooden manikins she had seen in art shop windows.

Jonathan stepped up to her and with a hand either side of her head tilted it to the angle he wanted.

"Hold that. Look straight ahead. Why are you shivering? For goodness' sake don't glare, try to look natural."

Rachel held what seemed to her to be an unnatural position until her buttocks felt dead. Not for anything would she complain. When it seemed she would fall apart he laid down the charcoal.

"There we are then. I've made several sketches. I think this one's the best." He screwed them all up but one. "You sat very well for a novice."

She glowed with pride and took the sketch from him. It was an excellent likeness. It was all there; the short dark hair, the huge, lustrous brown eyes, the small nose and round chin. A picture of youth and charm and innocence. Disappointed, she held it out to him.

"I'd like you to have it."

"Don't you like it?" he sounded surprised. She noticed one of his eyes was bloodshot and she hated herself for noticing.

"I think it's lovely. But you keep it. Please."

He took it and put it between the pages of a book and put the book on the shelves above the divan. Rachel smiled at her thoughts but suddenly afraid of wearing out her welcome, she thanked him and left.

She decided that would be the pattern of things. She would call on Miss Guilford first, do what she could to help her, then she would slip up the garden path to the studio. Her visits would be short, but they would be cheerful. He would begin to look forward to them; miss her when she didn't turn up.

There was still some heat in the sun when she arrived home so after making sure Rupert was nowhere about, she had a quick splash in the pool, went back to the house, showered and padded into her bedroom.

As she dried herself she looked in the full length mirror. Her face, neck, arms and legs were tanned a honey brown. The rest of her was magnolia coloured. She postured artistically then giggled.

"You are ridiculous," she told her reflection in an unusual burst of self-criticism. "Just look at you. Creamy white in the middle, brown round the edges. Like whipped cream walnut. And you're just as nutty."

Amy had come in from the garden. "Is that you Rachel? Who's up there with you?"

Rachel dressed quickly and went down-stairs. "I was thinking aloud. My book, you know."

"How is it coming along?"

"Oh—it's coming. It's all in my head but it will be good. I've been trying to paint too, but I'm hopeless."

"Ask Jonathan to help you. He won't mind."

Rachel smiled joyfully. "Perhaps I will."

"Have you fallen out with Rupert? We don't see so much of him these days."

"I'm playing tennis with him to-morrow." She decided not to tell Amy that Rupert was seeing rather a lot of Marilyn. When first David, then Mary and then Luke had told *her* the news, she had felt a little pang deep inside her. But then she decided it was none of her business.

Yet the following day when Rupert told her himself, a sense of desolation swept over her. Perhaps it was because he said what good fun Marilyn was when you got to know her.

"I suppose it depends what you want from life," she said loftily.

"What do you want from it Rachel?"

"Oh the usual things." She didn't want to talk to him about it.

"You won't find them with Jonathan Blake."

"Don't be silly Rupert."

"Silly? When you've talked of nothing else all the afternoon? Jonathan says this— Jonathan says that—anybody would think

171

he's the only one round here with any opinions the way you keep quoting him." He was silent for a moment or two, then, "You must be seeing a lot of him. Are you?"

Rachel bit back a sharp retort. Not for a moment would she concede it was any of his business. But he was a good friend, she did not want to hurt him. Did not want to say anything which would make him turn to a girl like Marilyn. The thought screwed her up inside.

"I asked you a question."

Rachel wriggled on the wooden seat and settled her back against the pavilion. She licked her ice-cream cornet and watched the children jostling for position round the ice-cream van. The plop and chunk of tennis balls against racket and court, the hum of insects and the chug of the grass-cutter in the distance all helped to soothe her irritation.

Once again she had fallen victim to Rupert's unreturnable service. It wouldn't have been so bad if he hadn't laughed at her frustrated attempts to return the ball. She had stomped off the court and bought herself an ice-cream. Rupert had followed suit, still chortling, and she had retaliated by talking about Jonathan. She had laid it on rather thickly. Poor Rupert. That cooled him.

"I'm sorry. What did you say? I was day dreaming."

"You always are. What do you dream about? Blake?"

"Don't be silly and don't call him Blake. You make him sound so ordinary."

"He is ordinary," growled Rupert. "An ordinary man with a talent for painting. Which is no more extraordinary than a man with a talent for plumbing or teaching. It's funny, but women never go overboard for *them*. Not in the same silly way I mean. It's the false glamour they fall for. A projection of their own minds. Women are masochists. They always fall for people who will hurt them."

"Aren't you jumping to conclusions Rupert? I haven't said—"

But Rupert hadn't finished. "I have another theory. Men like Blake are so self-centred that women regard it as a challenge. Their vanity won't let them accept that a man can be happy without them."

"That doesn't apply in Jonathan's case.

He adores women." Catching Rupert's shrewd glance she went on as though the idea were not torture to her. "He's had lots of affairs you know. Not that he talks about them but you can tell when you look at the portraits of some of the women he's painted. He brings out some quality in them—I don't know how to describe it." She concentrated her thoughts on the only one she had seen, the one of Lena. "He makes them look," she said thoughtfully, "as though they have just been passionately kissed."

Rupert snorted. "He isn't painting porn up there in that barn is he?"

She looked at him, her eyelids lowered in disdain. "I find the level of your conversation appallingly low."

"Well. I've heard girls talk rubbish before, but you're the limit."

Rachel sighed, finished her ice-cream and wiped her hands on her hanky. "That's the trouble with you youngsters, it's impossible to talk seriously about anything. Even art. You see everything in terms of sex."

"Yes. Well mind you don't." In a

different voice he said, "Have you ever posed for him—you know—in the—"

Unwilling to lie, determined not to tell the truth, Rachel smiled mysteriously. They were silent for a while then Rupert laughed.

"I've seen you naked you know."

Her mouth fell open and she stared at him. Rupert couldn't have seen her posing in front of her bedroom mirror, could he? From the garden? Birdwatching? Binoculars? Oh she'd never forgive him. *Never!* For once she was speechless.

"That shook you didn't it? do you know when it was?"

She dared not meet the laughter in his eyes. What a fool she'd feel if—

"You were about three and I was ten." Rupert chuckled. "You had a pot belly and your little bottom stuck out. It had the prettiest dimples. Have you still got—"

"Shut *up!*" She almost screamed at him in her relief and the next moment they were choking with laughter.

"I love you," said Rupert. The words came out suddenly as if of their own volition between one breath and another.

"Oh no!" Rachel stared at him in dismay.

"What's so terrible about it?"

He tried to take her hand, she snatched it away. She knew she should have been prepared for this, despite Marilyn. Now and again there was something in Rupert's attitude towards her which made her suspect that however many setbacks he suffered, however long he had to wait, he would win in the end. She had recognised it and although it had pleased her in one sense, it had irritated her, too.

"You must have known," Rupert was saying quietly. "You women have an instinct about this sort of thing."

Grateful as she was for "you women" the rest of the sentence hardly penetrated. She did not love him. Therefore she could not accept that he could care for her. Yet she revelled in his admiration.

And then the thought came to her. Perhaps Rupert was suffering over her as she herself was suffering for Jonathan? A wave of compassion swept over her.

"I'm sorry Rupert dear," she said at last. "I'm terribly fond of you but I don't love you. Not enough to marry you. I *am* sorry."

Rupert bit off the bottom of his cornet and sucked the ice-cream from the narrow end.

"Who said anything about marriage?"

She stared at him. "You're not suggesting—?"

"There's no need to sound so angry. I'm not suggesting anything. All I said was 'I love you'."

"But—"

"But nothing. I love you. Full stop. Whether I could bear to spend the rest of my life with you is something I shall have to think about very carefully."

And to think she had felt sorry for him!

"Oh me too. I mean. Fancy waking up in the middle of the night and seeing *that* on the next pillow." She made a derogatory gesture towards his flaming hair.

"You sleep with the light on?"

"No. But you do. At least it was on at four o'clock twice this week. I saw it from my bedroom window."

"You must have been leaning out a long way."

"I was—" She bit her lip as she realised what this implied.

"Hm!" Rupert shook his head doubtfully. "I'm very flattered, but I don't think I could marry a woman who spends her days yearning for one man and her nights gazing at the bedroom of another one. Shows a marked instability of character."

Rachel glowered at him. "When you have made up your mind you will let me know, won't you?"

"You'll be the first to hear. Would you like another ice-cream?"

"No thank you."

"Right. Let's go." He stood in front of her, smiling and holding out his hand.

After a slight hesitation she took it and they walked away swinging their clasped hands like children.

10

ON the day of the garden fete Rachel woke to grey skies, damp patches in the garden and a cool breeze ruffling the puddles.

"Would you believe it! After all the lovely weather we've had—"

Amy smiled comfortably. "Rain before seven, fine before eleven," she said. "And if you are going to be throwing tables and trestles around this morning you'd better get some food into you."

"Oh Amy! Liver and fried onions! That's enough darling. You'll have me as podgy as Marilyn."

"Marilyn?" Amy looked at her in surprise. "Get away with you. She's got a bit more bust than you but I wouldn't call her podgy."

Rachel ate in silence for a while. "She isn't really. It's a sort of impression she gives lately. It's her face more than anything, I think. You know, puffy. As though she isn't too well. I can't understand her.

Some days she's quite friendly with me when I go in the shop and another time she won't speak to me."

"Hm. Trouble at home probably. Makes her moody. That brother of hers must be a trial to live with. Always in and out of court. And of course, Marilyn is out late every night with one young man or another, so I'm told. You can't keep that up even at her age."

She looked at the clock. "I don't want to hurry you love, but it's time you weren't here. I'm surprised Rupert hasn't called for you. He's helping too, isn't he?"

Rachel folded her napkin, brushed a few crumbs across the table with her fingers, then sat very still for a moment.

"Amy, did you know that Rupert has been seeing quite a lot of Marilyn lately? Ever since the car rocking incident I told you about? Remember?" Amy nodded. "That's over six weeks ago. If she was out late last night he was too. They went to a club in Nottingham. I heard Rupert's banger come down the road at well after two o'clock—"

"Oh Rachel!"

"Don't look at me like that Amy. It's not my fault."

"Are you sure?"

"Of course I'm sure. I'm not Rupert's keeper."

"No. But you did say—I mean, you gave me the impression, a few weeks ago that you—oh well, it's none of my business. But Rupert's a nice boy. I don't like to see him throwing himself away on a girl like her."

"He's old enough to please himself. He says Marilyn's good fun. I think they are very well matched. Both rather immature."

Amy smiled and shook her head but then her expression changed. It became keener, more searching.

Rachel knew what she was thinking. She returned the stare and winked solemnly. "Don't worry darling. Rupert's nobody's fool. He gives the impression that life isn't to be taken seriously, but underneath the banter you can sense tremendous strength. He'll make out all right."

The next moment she was wondering at herself. At the contradictory statements she had made about Rupert in the last few minutes. Which did she believe? Amy was watching her carefully.

Rachel laughed self-consciously and said, "I reek of fried onions."

"Get along with you. Have a drink of milk." A shaft of sunlight slid along the wall. "There you are. I told you it would turn out fine. It's going to be a lovely day."

Mrs. Kaye was unusually grumpy. "I took Rupert a cup of tea at seven o'clock but he won't get up—"

"You did *what!*" Rachel was horrified. "May I go up."

"If you like. Turn left at the top of the stairs. His room is the second one."

Rachel bounded up the stairs, flung open the door and marched up to the bed. Vaguely, she was aware of a pleasant room with its masses of books, the desk and old library chair under the window, the Peter Scott prints on the wall.

"Out!" she demanded, tugging at the bed-clothes. Just as Rupert was about to be revealed in all his pink and white nakedness, he made a grab.

"Hey! What about my dignity?"

"You haven't got any. Come on. You're supposed to be plaiting the maypole this morning."

"Bring it up. I'll plait it here. Ooh! my head!" He buried his head in his arms.

"Serves you right." Rachel turned her back. "I'll count up to twenty. If you aren't out of bed by then—one—two—three—" The bed creaked. "Four—five—"

"Not so fast. I'm out of bed but I've lost my underpants. Hold on a minute, the clean ones are in the drawer in front of you."

She heard him padding round the bed towards her, half turned her head, saw his reflection in the full length mirror.

She fled downstairs.

By the time they reached the meadow where the Garden Fete was to be held, people were already banging about with hammers, getting in each other's way, harassing the shirt-sleeved rector.

The beer tent was up. Rupert and David humped crates of beer about while Rachel and Mary Hornsby sorted out the things they had been given for their stall—

costume jewellery, toast-racks, pottery, books.

Mrs. Jakes waddled by, her cigarette leading the way. She turned and peered at the girls and her fat chin wobbled as she manoeuvred the cigarette from one side of her mouth to the other.

"How's the painting coming along dear?" she asked Rachel.

"What painting?" Rachel paused in mid-swoop on a bundle of books under the stall.

"Having painting lessons aren't you? With J.B.? I've seen you up at the studio several times a week and I know he's not painting your portrait else I'd have seen it when I cleaned. So I said to myself, 'He must be giving her lessons'. I mean you wouldn't spend all that time with him without good reason now, would you? I did think at first he might be using you as a model, Mrs. Sefton not being able to get down because of her little boy's illness—"

Rachel looked at her angrily. For one thing, she had not been able to find out why Lena was so rarely at the studio these last few weeks. But only because she was too proud to ask Jonathan. That was one reason. Actually, she had managed to convince herself that he had ended the association now that the portrait was finished and she dared not ask in case the illusion was shattered. And now Mrs. Jakes had shattered it.

"You mustn't mind me saying this dear, but I think you are being very silly. People are bound to think the worst you know. A man old enough to be your father. I'm telling you for your own good dear. I believe in speaking my own mind—"

"But unfortunately you can't do that without revealing a very unpleasant facet of it, Mrs. Jakes," said Mary. "Now will you excuse us? We have a lot to do. Mind you don't set yourself on fire." She looked pointedly at the length of ash which trembled on the end of Mrs. Jakes's cigarette and then fell on to the front of her dress.

The woman glared at her, threw the stub into the grass and walked away.

Mary ground out the light with her heel. "Stupid woman," she muttered. "Come on Rachel, let's go and see how the chaps are getting on."

Rupert and David were unpacking

glasses which the rector and his wife were polishing. Mary took another cloth and started to help. Rachel went to the far end of the tent where it was dim and quiet. She pretended to look for another cloth but all she wanted was somewhere to hide.

She had told Rupert she did not care if people said nasty things about her, but she did. It made her feel shameful and cheap. And it was so unfair. Her visits to the studio were quite innocent. All she and Jonathan did was talk. The door was always open, anybody could walk in on them, he took good care of that.

Rachel leaned against the tent pole, her right foot gently rubbing the back of her other leg.

"'Lo Rachel," said a voice. "Whasser-matter? Why are you looking so glum?" The words were slurred.

Rachel started violently and turned to find Henry Sefton in the other corner of the tent, sitting on an upturned crate.

"Hello Mr. Sefton. I didn't see you. Was I looking glum? Perhaps it's because I'm hungry." She walked over to him. "How are you? I haven't seen you for ages.

Not since you gave Jonathan and me a lift to the station."

She was talking fast, relieved to get away from her thoughts. Henry was drinking. He had a flask by his side and an almost empty glass in his hand. From his slurred speech and the difficulty he seemed to be having keeping his eyes focused on Rachel, she guessed he'd been at it for some time.

"Is Lena coming this afternoon?"

He nodded. "Sh'll look in for a minute —like royalty. But not till later. Gone to take the boy to Wh—Whatstandwell. Camping." He made heavy weather of the name but got somewhere near it. "Been ill. The boy. Better now. Good mother— no good wife. The lady of the manor—"

His speech got worse. Rachel started to move away but Mrs. Jakes and one or two of her friends were standing near the exit. Rachel decided to stay where she was rather than pass them.

Henry refilled his glass and drank deeply. "My wife—crazy 'bout her. She don' care a fig for me." He said this in a tone of deep surprise with his eyes wide open as he looked at Rachel. "My own

187

fault—let her have her own way too much —been unfaithful for years—but I love her so I said nothing—Love her—have her on any terms—"

He began to tremble violently. His hand fumbled with a button on his jacket then fell helplessly to his side. "Trapped," he said. "Love's a trap. No way out—have her on any terms."

The tears came into his eyes and brimmed over. Rachel was filled with pity for him and for the first time she saw Jonathan Blake through cool, critical eyes. He was the cause of this man's misery.

The mood was gone in a flash. Of course not, Lena was the cause. She had both men where she wanted them. Her husband through his love for her and Jonathan through the love of his work, his studio and the home and friends he had made for himself in Lynbury. For if he did not toe the line, Lena's line, she would evict him, and all the land would go to the speculators who wanted to destroy the village by turning it into one big housing estate.

Someone grasped her arm. "Come and get a bit of lunch before the rush starts," said Rupert. He looked at Henry. "Want

188

me to take you home old chap? You don't look very well."

Henry shook his head. Straightening his shoulders with a tremendous effort, he gave them a glimpse of himself as he used to be. "Thank you Rupert, for your concern. I'm quite all right. Really. Goodbye Rachel, it's been nice talking to you." He shook hands with them and walked away.

"Hm!" said Rupert. "I thought he was pickled—"

Rachel did not answer.

By the middle of the afternoon she and Mary had sold all the articles on their stall. Rachel had played table skittles, guessed the weight of a cake, watched the infants dancing round the maypole and now she was drinking tea and wondering why Jonathan had not turned up.

It was a bright sunny afternoon as Amy had predicted, but to Rachel it was dull and colourless. Were Jonathan and Lena together up at the studio? Whatstandwell wasn't far away, she could have been back ages ago. Had she gone to see him? Were they taking advantage of the fact that Henry was at the fete? Were they making up for the time they had lost through the illness of Lena's little boy?

Suddenly two hands came from behind and covered her eyes. Jonathan? Her heart beat wildly. No. It wasn't the kind of thing he would do in public. There was a smell of tobacco on the fingers so it wasn't Rupert or David.

The hands were removed and the next moment Luke was by her side sitting straddle legged on the bench.

"Didn't expect to see me here did you?" His dark, handsome face was eager; his eyes looked hopefully, expectantly into hers. He reminded Rachel of a faithful dog waiting to be patted and called "Good Boy".

She looked at him in mock severity. "Just like you to come when all the work's finished. Why didn't you come this morning and help with the heavy stuff?"

"Who me? I was in bed. Told you I'm on nights reg'lar. Anyway," he glanced around, his eyes full of contempt. "This ain't my scene. Got no time for church folk, they only want you for what they can get out of you. Tell you what though—" He sidled a little closer to Rachel. "I'll help to take it all down if you'll come out wi' me after. I'll work like stink. Honest. Will you? We'll go anywhere you like. Pictures. Dancing. We could have a run to Matlock on the bike—or anywhere. You've only got to say. What about it, aye?"

Rachel's smile faded. The boy's face was full of devotion, or was it desire? How could she make him see he was wasting his time? He was an unnecessary complication in her life and she wished he would leave her alone. He mixed her up. Because if she were indifferent to him, how was it she cared whether she hurt him or not? And why was life so unfair. All she wanted was Jonathan. Like Henry with Lena, she would take him on any terms, yet because of the stupid difference in their ages—

"Luke," she said gently, "I like you but I don't want to go out with you and I wish you wouldn't ask me again. It wouldn't be fair. There's somebody else you see."

"What here? In Lynbury? Some hopes you got." His face was full of disbelief. And then it cleared. "You don't mean Rupert Kaye?" He settled back and folded his arms. "Ah well! You've had it then haven't you? You had your chance there didn't you? And wouldn't have none of it. He's makin' it wi' Marilyn now, didn't you know? Boy! That's some doll! Hey! Shall I tell you what she—"

"I don't want to hear anything about it," snapped Rachel. Despite herself, her stomach turned over at the thought of Rupert and Marilyn—at the thought of the lewdness in Luke's eyes and voice as he spoke of them. Was this how people spoke of her and Jonathan?

Luke was looking at her curiously. "Sorry duck," he said at last. "Thought you'd passed him on. I mean, you didn't want him, did you, when you'd got him?" He studied her a moment longer. "You can't blame him you know. Marilyn's great. Just great. It was a toss-up between you and her for me—but you have the edge on her 'cos you talk nice. Fraightfully upper clarss. When you say 'what?' like that, 'what?' it sounds plummy. Yet when Marilyn says 'what' it just sounds common. I don't know why."

He sighed. "P'raps that's what you don't like about me? I sound common don't I? But a lot of people are coming round to my way of talking. On telly, everywhere." He thought about it for a while. "I could go to night school. Learn English. For you I'd—"

"Oh Luke, *Luke*." Rachel sighed, smiled and shook her head. "It's nothing to do with that. It's just—" she lifted her hands and let them fall into her lap. A gesture of hopelessness.

Luke lifted one into his great paw and held it lightly. She frowned at the nicotine-stained fingers, the beautiful nails which were rimmed with dirt as though they were in mourning. Had he never been taught to use a nail-brush?

As though he read her thoughts he dropped her hand, took a match from his pocket and began poking at the dirt in his nails. It was not very effective. Rachel watched as with his strong thumb-nail he whittled the match-stick to a point and began again. Suddenly, he tossed the match away.

"Anyway," he said. "What's a bit o' muck? It's here," he thumped his chest. "It's what you got in here that matters. That's what counts." His face was an

193

offended mask. He got up and started to walk away then he turned.

"Tell me straight out—is it Rupert Kaye you want? 'Cos I've only got to crook my little finger and Marilyn'll come runnin'." He looked at Rachel, his eyes full of speculation. "Reckon she could teach you a thing or two at that. Got real blood in her veins has Marilyn, not iced water." He stood looking at her. "What d'you say? Want me to get him off the hook for you?"

She smiled at his arrogance. "Thank you for your offer, Luke. But Rupert and I are more like brother and sister. We've known each other since we were children."

"Well there's nobody else round here." His expression turned surly. "I'll tell you what it is. You're a snob. And let me tell you something. While I've got these," he held up his hands, fingers spread wide. "While I've got these, I'm the equal of any man in England."

He was waving his hands in front of her face now, and she could see his temper beginning to get the better of him. He looked quite ugly. She made a tentative movement away from him but he held her shoulder and pushed her back again. "You're a rotten little snob," he repeated. "And do you know somethin'? Them as thinks the workin' class is below 'em, gets left on the shelf like your Aunt Amy. Think on that, Miss Toffee Nose."

He gave her another push then turned and stomped into the beer tent.

Rachel stared after him, her breath of relief blowing out her lips and cheeks, the nonsensical remark about Amy buried in a welter of confusing thoughts. How could you judge people? What yard-stick did you apply? Was Luke a bad-mannered oaf with a surface charm which he switched on to get his own way? Or was he fundamentally a nice boy striking back in the only way he knew, because he was hurt? And how was she going to write a book about people if she did not understand them? Take Rupert. On the surface, immature and easy-going. Yet on a deeper level, she could not keep up with him.

And Jonathan? Mature, handsome, trendy. An interesting talker. But what of the man beneath? She did not know. She did not care. But she ached for the sight of him. Why didn't he come?

She sat a little while longer and breathed a sigh of relief as she heard the distinctive roar of Luke's motor bike revving up in the car park. She concentrated on the sound. The engine was quieter as he weaved his way in and out between cars and people passing through the gate into the meadow. It roared again as he passed through Lower Lynbury. In her imagination she followed him down the main street on to the by-pass.

The sound died away. Rachel got up and fetched a tray of tea and cakes which she took across to David and Mary who were in charge of the children's treasure trove. She could not rid her mind of the things Luke had said.

"David, am I a snob?"

"I hope so ducky. After all it's only another way of saying your standards are high. Thank God. I mean, where would we be if everybody settled for the mediocre? There'd be precious little progress."

Mary laughed. "I don't think you are on Rachel's wavelength, David. It's Luke, isn't it?" she asked Rachel. "Won't take no for an answer?"

Rachel nodded.

"I thought so. The local girls have spoiled him. He can't believe anyone can resist him."

"Marilyn seems able to. She and Rupert are going strong, according to Luke." Rachel sounded a little too nonchalant even to her own ears.

"Serves you right. It's your own fault."

"David!"

"Well it is. Ooh! you try my patience sometimes, Rachel. Can't see what's right under your own nose. Nice chap like Rupert and you throw him to a girl like *her*. You'll be sorry if he marries her."

Mary laughed. "So will Rupert. But you can't blame Rachel. Rupert's old enough to please himself. Personally, I think Marilyn's trying to make Luke jealous. I'm sure he's the one she really wants." Her eyes met Rachel's and the message came across clearly. "I know you care more than you will admit."

"Whee-whee. Whee-whee!" The children had stopped digging in the sand for buried treasure and were echoing the wail of the siren which was wafted to them over the noise of the crowd.

197

The three young adults looked at one another in momentary apprehension.

"Road accident! Oh God!" said Rachel, her face whitening as she thought of Luke tearing along the bypass on his motor bike. *In a temper caused by her.*

"Marilyn's brother breaking into a bank," David and Mary spoke in unison. They laughed and the children began digging again.

"I wonder why Marilyn doesn't leave home. It must be awful living in the same house with someone who's always in trouble with the police." Rachel spoke for the sake of something to say. "Are her parents dependent on her?"

"She left once, about a year ago but according to Marilyn her brother fetched her back and gave her a sound beating. Said she could leave to get married, but until then her place was with her parents."

"The stuff of Victorian melodrama in a place like Lynbury?" Rachel said with a laugh. "What next?"

"You find it everywhere. Usually in greater concentration in smaller towns and villages," said David. "You'd be surprised at the things people tell me. I could write a book."

"As a matter of fact, David, I *am* writing one. Well—I haven't actually put pen to paper but it's all here." She tapped her forehead. "It's only a matter of finding the time to write it down." She picked up the tea tray.

"If you sell the film rights you will invite us to the premiere won't you?"

"Of course. Put your cups on here, I'll take them to the litter bin for you."

"Bless you. Thanks for the tea, ducky." As she walked away he said to Mary, "I love Rachel dearly, but she has a touch of the Walter Mitty's."

"So I've noticed," said Mary.

"I heard that, David Ramsey," called Rachel.

"You were meant to ducky."

Their laughter was cut short by a feeling of tension which was sweeping over the crowd like a tidal wave. Two more cars had arrived. The occupants spread the news of the crash half a mile down the by-pass. A motor cyclist and a car. Yes. Fatal.

The words passed from group to group. Teacups were forgotten, darts were poised in mid-throw. A table skittle rocked and fell. Who? The question hung in the air as people tried to remember what sons and daughters, friends and neighbours were doing that afternoon.

Rachel knew. The motor cyclist was Luke. He had driven away in a temper because she had upset him.

Her legs began to tremble. Silently, with bleached face and pinched-up nose, she stood listening to the reports.

Another car arrived. More details. A motor cyclist speeding along had lost control on the bend and collided with a car coming in the opposite direction. Driver killed outright.

Rachel had a vision of Luke as she had last seen him. Not in a temper. Moments before that. Young, eager, full of life. She fought a rising nausea and then heard someone say "—No. Motor cyclist was thrown clear. He finished up in the ditch. He was wearing his crash helmet and though he was in a bloody mess, literally, he was conscious, and judging by his language, he'd be all right."

Oh thank God!

"—But the car driver died instantly. Multiple injuries."

So she had something to answer for? A faint moan came from Rachel. Mary and David helped her into the tea tent.

"Find Rupert," Mary whispered to David. Apart from the two girls the tent was empty. Everybody else was outside talking about the accident.

And so they were the only ones who did not see the Panda car arrive in the meadow. Did not see the two policemen walking between the stalls asking for Henry Sefton.

Did not see them coax a befuddled Henry from the beer tent into the police car and whisk him off to identify the dead driver of the wrecked car.

The dead woman driver. Lena Sefton.

11

IT was a week after the funeral. Henry, who could have been forgiven had he drunk himself paralytic, was stone cold sober with a hatred in his heart equally cold and hard.

His hatred was not for Luke who had caused the accident, but was turned full on Jonathan Blake who had been in the car with Lena and who had escaped with cuts, bruises and shock.

Luke, his right leg encased in plaster, his handsome face stitched up in two places, was still in hospital. From there he had written a sincere and humble letter to Henry. In it he said how much he admired Mrs. Sefton and how it bugged him to think he had caused her death. He blamed himself, was willing to take any punishment "the beaks decided to dole out" and Henry was welcome to use his letter in any way he thought fit.

Henry responded magnificently. He sent Luke a bottle of champagne and a note to the effect that he must not blame himself entirely. There were contributory factors of which Luke could not be aware.

Rachel was shown Henry's note when she visited Luke. She had gone into the ward white-faced and apprehensive; ready to take all the blame for putting him in a bad mood and thereby indirectly causing the accident. She had got to the point where she believed she would be willing to sacrifice herself in atonement. Well, almost.

Luke was propped up in bed, one leg in traction. He was surrounded by pretty nurses, enjoying the party atmosphere generated by Henry's champagne. His greeting was casual.

"Hi there Rachel! Want a sup? Help yourself if you can find anything to drink out of." He showed her Henry's letter then carried on his flirtation with a pretty, giggling Jamaican who was trying to take his temperature.

Rachel put down the cigarettes and the magazines she had brought him, and crept away.

"I wonder what Henry meant by 'contributory factors'," Mary said later when she, Rachel and David were in the workroom together. Mary was making coffee, David cutting out, while Mary's twins played quietly in a corner with an assortment of buttons and beads.

"Lena didn't drink," Mary went on almost as if she were talking to herself. "At least not enough to affect her driving, which you always said was very good, David!"

He nodded. "She was proud of her driving. Good enough to have taken avoiding action if she'd wanted to—even on that rotten bend. Remember Rupert's banger running off the road there? Nasty stretch that. All the same—"

If she'd wanted to? Rachel stared at David. He refused to look at her.

"David. Do you know something we don't?"

He flushed and pushed at his hair which he wore much shorter these days, in a style which went well with his more sober outfits.

"I only know what Mrs. Jakes told me. She's been looking after J.B. since the accident. Cooking as well as cleaning."

"Don't I know it?" grumbled Rachel.

"She wouldn't let me in to see him. I told her Amy had sent me and she said 'Tell Amy to come herself'. She practically shut the door in my face."

"Yes—well. Amy and J.B. were pretty good friends at one time."

"They still are, but you know Amy. She's on so many committees and things, she's hardly ever in. But you were saying—?"

"I was saying I only know what Mrs. Jakes told me. It appears that every day since the accident Henry has strolled down as far as the studio and stood leaning on the fence. Just looking. It got on J.B.'s nerves and yesterday he asked Henry why the hell he didn't come in and say what he had to say." David took the cup of coffee Mary was holding out, sipped it and went on.

"According to Mrs. Jakes, Henry went in but didn't speak for a long time. She was in the kitchen and as you know the internal walls are only plywood, so it was like being in the same room as Henry and J.B. Well, she could hear Henry walking about as though he was looking at the paintings. All at once he said, 'Where is it?' 'Where's what?' Jonathan asked. 'Where's my wife's portrait? I want it'."

"Mrs. Jakes said there was a silence you could feel, and J.B. told Henry he could have it at a price and on condition he submitted it to the Academy."

David sipped his coffee again and turned to one of the children who was holding up something for him to look at. He made a kissing noise at the child and then turned back to Rachel and Mary.

"Henry said he wouldn't pay for the portrait and it would be shown publicly over his dead body. Ever so nasty, he was, Mrs. Jakes says."

Rachel sighed. "I can see Henry's point of view but it's not just a portrait of a nude. It's beautiful. A true work of art. He might be proud—"

David ignored her interruption. "Mrs. Jakes said they had a terrible row, with Henry saying he wished he had killed J.B. two years ago when he first broke up the marriage, and J.B. saying if it hadn't been him it would have been somebody else because Lena was that sort. Henry called him a fornicator, said he was using the studio for immoral purposes, called him a defiler of young girls—"

Rachel blinked and felt herself shrink a little at this.

David said, "Of course, we don't know how much Mrs. Jakes heard and how much she made up herself, but I do believe her when she says Henry gave J.B. his marching orders, because that's what he'd have done ages ago if it hadn't been for Lena. But J.B. took the wind out of his sails by telling Henry he was leaving anyway. All the arrangements had been made and he was only waiting for the portrait to dry hard enough to send to his agent in London, then he's going to live in Rome."

"Rome!" The word was forced from Rachel's stiff lips. She stared at David who went on talking as though he had not heard the overtones of agony in her voice.

"He's got everything fixed. It was all arranged when he was there in the spring. Didn't he tell you Rachel?" David was probing her wound deliberately. Not out of cruelty or spite, she was sure of that. He was twisting the knife, seeking out the rotten parts so that it would heal more quickly.

Mary gave him a warning look. "I expect he kept it dark because he knew what a scene Lena would make. You can't blame him—" She poured more coffee into Rachel's cup. "How did Henry take the news?"

"Well, by now, Mrs. Jakes stood in the doorway watching them, and she said Henry stared at J.B. and asked him if Lena knew. When J.B. said she did, Henry went as white as a sheet and asked him when he had told her. And then it all came out."

David paused for effect.

"He told her that afternoon? In the car?" Mary sat very still as she asked the question.

David nodded. "A few minutes before the accident apparently."

"Oh—" The sound, breathy and long drawn out, came from both girls.

"J.B. told Henry that Lena refused to believe him at first. And then she started to argue and threaten to follow him wherever he went. He told her to shut up and concentrate on her driving, and she flew into a temper. Something she never does normally when she's behind the wheel," David said. "Well, one thing led to another, but once she realised he meant to go, she started to sob. He begged her to stop the car but she took no notice. Drove faster if anything. Couldn't stop crying. Took the bend wider than she should. Luke, coming hell for leather the other way saw this car heading straight for him, panicked, lost control and went bang into it."

There was a horrified silence. After it, Mary said, "So technically, it was as much Lena's fault as Luke's?"

"Not according to the inquest. Lena was just inside the white line, Luke was over it. Personally, I'm inclined to agree with Henry. It was J.B.'s fault for choosing such a bloody silly time to tell her. Knowing what she was like. Sorry girls, don't often let rip—"

"Did these domestic details come out at the inquest David?" Mary asked the question but she was watching Rachel anxiously.

"You bet they didn't. J.B. was the only one who knew what a state Lena was in and why but he wasn't likely to tell. He wouldn't risk his name being dragged in the dirt. Not that it would have served any useful purpose—"

"Mightn't it have made it easier for Luke when his case comes up?"

"Perhaps. Who knows? I told you before," David looked directly at Rachel now. "J.B. is a taker. He'll do what's best for number one always." He smiled at her, as though the words had no special significance for her.

Rachel sat a moment longer then she stumbled to her feet. "I'd better get Amy's shopping. She'll wonder where I've got to. See you. Thanks for the coffee."

As she went down the stairs, the pain was more than she could bear. Was this how Lena had felt? Had she died because her eyes were blinded by tears or had she deliberately ignored the oncoming motor bike?

Either way, it was something Jonathan would carry on his conscience for the rest of his life. Nobody seemed to think of that. And it wasn't his fault Lena had fallen so madly in love with him. He couldn't help that any more than he could help Rachel herself—her thoughts broke off. She dared not carry the parallel too far.

By the time she reached the shopping precinct, Rachel had convinced herself that it was different in her case. *She* hadn't thrown herself at Jonathan. The initiative had always been his. The hand-holding in the tea-shop (for that's how she saw it now) the invitation to accompany him on a sketching trip. The kiss. The invitation to his studio. Everything. They had become tremendous friends—

Oh yes? said her common sense. So why didn't he tell you he was going away?

Rachel stood looking in a tool-shop window while she thought that one out. But she saw nothing of the planes and drills and screwdrivers. She was desolate. Why hadn't he told her? And then a blinding thought struck. There could be only one reason. He was going for *her* sake! Because he could no longer fight his love for her. He was taking the only sensible (to him) way out, because of the difference in their ages.

Oh!

She looked at the window, seeing

nothing, not even her own reflection. Her tangled nerves relaxed. The desolation was replaced by a warm glow. Her eyes pricked with tears. Poor Jonathan.

She must not let him do it. How could she stop him? How could she persuade him that the difference in their ages did not matter one jot?

She turned away from the window. Somebody bumped into her but she hardly noticed. There wasn't a great deal of time—

She tried to think of the great women of history and how they had used their feminine wiles to influence the men they had loved. Not one name sprang to mind. All the historical novels she had read; the modern ones—were they all wasted on her? Had she learned nothing from them?

She wandered round the library, seeking inspiration. Found none. She finished her shopping in a trance-like state. Little wisps of doubt were pushed away.

Amy's voice weeks ago, when they were talking about something Henry Sefton had said at David's party "you read far too much into the things people say—you mustn't let your imagination run away with you—you will cause a lot of trouble for yourself one of these days—"

She had not imagined that kiss in the Derbyshire inn. Nor the fact that for weeks afterwards, Jonathan had avoided her. Deliberately avoided her. A man, a *mature* man like him did not behave like that to a woman about whom he was indifferent. She *couldn't* believe it meant nothing to him.

Another memory stabbed. David Ramsey's voice at the Garden Fete "—Rachel has a touch of the Walter Mitty's."

She knew and recognised this trait in her character. She was a dreamer. But she had not dreamed up the expression in Jonathan's eyes when he looked at her. The way he tried to avoid touching her. His refusal to paint her portrait. It was obvious. He could not trust his feelings.

Still in a daze, she stood on the bridge on her way home, gazing at the studio and wondering how much longer Mrs. Jakes would be in charge.

As she stood, she became aware of a lonely looking figure down by the river, sitting with its back to a tree. Marilyn.

There was something so dejected about the girl's posture that Rachel followed an impulse and walked down to her.

"Hi!" said Marilyn after a brief glance. She went on shredding a dock leaf.

Rachel sat down beside her. "I went to see Luke, in hospital. He sends his love." This wasn't true but Rachel thought Marilyn might like to hear it. She shut out of her mind a picture of Luke surrounded by pretty nurses. "I don't suppose you have much time for visiting?"

Marilyn shrugged. "Oh *him*," she said sulkily.

Rachel looked at the puffy face. "You look a bit under the weather. I suppose it's this heat," she went on when Marilyn didn't answer. "It's enough to get anybody down."

Still no answer. Marilyn crossed one bare leg over the other. She was wearing sandals and Rachel saw the silver varnish on her toe nails was chipped and cracked. So was that on her fingers. A grubby shoulder strap had slipped and was showing beneath her sleeveless frock. But Marilyn herself, thought Rachel, if you disregarded the slight puffiness, was uncommonly pretty. She had deep blue eyes, a fine skin and soft fair hair which she wore at shoulder length. What had Rupert said? "Great fun, Marilyn." And Luke? "Some doll, that. She could teach you a thing or two. Got warm blood in her veins, not iced water."

What, she wondered, would Marilyn do about Jonathan if she were in my place? Pity she wasn't the sort of girl you could confide in. Goodness, what wouldn't she give for a chat with a girl friend her own age. Someone who would help her to get things in perspective.

And then she noticed the bruise. Marilyn's frock had a scooped-out neckline and she was sitting so that the back of the frock fell away from her body.

"Rough night last night?" she asked lightly.

Marilyn glared. "What are you gettin' at?"

"You have a great bruise on your back. I thought perhaps—"

"Well don't."

There was a long, difficult silence. Rachel was on the point of leaving when Marilyn spoke.

"As a matter of fact, me brother did it."

"Your brother? Why?"

"'Cos he's a thug, that's why. A great big, bullying thug."

Rachel waited for a moment then said gently, "Do you have to live at home? I mean, you could get a job anywhere and lots of girls share flats these days." Then she laughed. "Hark at me. My parent's wouldn't let me. Perhaps yours—?" She waited, looking at Marilyn.

"They couldn't stop me if they wanted to. I'm over age. I went once but I came back. I missed me Mam and Dad. I mean, why should I leave them and all me pals just for *him*. No thank you. I got as much right to live here as he has."

Rachel remembered something she had heard Mary say. "You came back because you wanted to? Not because your brother made you?"

Marilyn gave her a sly look out of the corner of her eyes. "Who you been talking to?" Then she laughed. "Folks'll believe anything you tell 'em if it fits in wi' what they think about you." Then the laughter died. "Nobody pushes me around. Nobody. Least of all our kid." She turned away as though that were the end of the conversation. Yet Rachel had an uncanny feeling Marilyn did not want her to go away. That she had something to tell her.

The surliness was receding. Smugness was taking its place.

A triumphant smugness. Yet there was also something secretive in Marilyn's manner.

The silence went on. Rachel turned her head away and watched people passing over the bridge. She became conscious of the sounds from the colliery, something she hardly noticed nowadays. A sparrow landed a few feet away and flew off again swiftly. Rachel's thoughts were with Jonathan.

"—I wasn't going to tell anybody yet. Not till I'm sure. But it's nice to talk to somebody your own age. An' I'm *pretty* sure now—"

"Hm? What? I'm sorry. I was miles away. What were you saying?"

"I said I missed last month. An' if it don't come tomorrow as it should, I reckon I'm preggy." Marilyn's lip trembled despite her casual tone.

Rachel stared blankly. "Preggy? *Pregnant*? Oh God! No! Oh poor Marilyn."

"Oh poor Marilyn!" mimicked Marilyn.

Rachel stared at her. Silly, feckless, vulnerable. And failed to see her own reflection. But Marilyn went out with lots of boys, she thought, and before she could stop herself, she asked. "Do you know who—whose—?"

Marilyn's face flamed. She turned tearful, mascara-blotched but indignant eyes on her.

"What the hell d'you mean by that? Of course I know! I'm not promishus and don't try to make out I am—"

"Promiscuous," corrected Rachel absently. Her sympathies were with Marilyn but her thoughts were elsewhere. She started to shiver. Looking down at her arms she noticed they were goose-pimpled.

Marilyn had dried her tears and was prattling on about where she would live once they were married.

"What will your parents say?" interrupted Rachel.

"Look. I keep on telling you I'm over age. This is my business and nobody else's. I'm—aye," she looked suspiciously at Rachel. "How old do you think I am?"

"About my age. Sixteen." Rachel said absently.

Marilyn gave a snort of amusement. Not altogether displeased.

"I'm twenty-two. I'll be twenty-three at Christmas."

Rachel stared in disbelief.

"Gospel," said Marilyn. The sly look came back. She looked at Rachel for several seconds before she spoke again.

"So you see," she said. And her voice was smooth, like silk. "It's nobody's business but mine." She waited. "And Rupert Kaye's," she added.

Disbelief, a nagging feeling unrecognisable as jealousy; disgust. All the emotions followed one another and left their mark on Rachel's face.

"You look a bit green. What's up? Been making it wi' you as well has he?" Marilyn smirked triumphantly, then her eyes narrowed as she looked at Rachel's slim waist. "Well well! But I got first claim now you know." She laughed raucously. "God knows what Mama Kaye will have to say about this. But if she don't like it she'll have to lump it."

Rachel's mouth was so dry she couldn't speak. Rupert! It couldn't be true. Why not? her reason asked. He was young, full of life. Marilyn was pretty, she knew how to attract men. Rupert had reacted normally. Why shouldn't he?

She caught the gleam of mischief in Marilyn's eye.

"I don't believe you. Not Rupert."

"Why not? He's a man i'n't he?" Marilyn's tone registered genuine surprise. Suddenly she laughed out loud. "D'you know—I've often wondered about you and" she nodded towards the studio, "and him. Jonathan Blake. I've often wondered if you managed to get him bedded down. I know now. You haven't. And should I tell you why?" She sat up and for the first time looked straight into Rachel's eyes. "I'll tell you why. It's because you don't know the first thing about men. You've got about as much sex appeal as a bag of frozen peas. Do you know what? His sort are the easiest of the lot. If you can't get him you've had it." She laughed, a rich, raw sound, full of derision. It echoed up and down the valley. "Or should I say you *haven't* had it? An' never will—"

But Rachel, trembling with rage, humiliation and something else, an emotion she could not define, was walking away.

Blindly she pushed her way between a gang of sub-teenagers playing with a ball on the path at the side of the meadow. Not until she was near the top of the hill where she and Rupert often sat did she get control of her thoughts.

One moment the misery and grief caused by Marilyn's disclosure about her pregnancy was uppermost; the next she was writhing in humiliation as she remembered how Marilyn had jeered at her "failure" with Jonathan. And to make it worse, the things Marilyn had said, "you have as much sex appeal as a bag of frozen peas", "you don't know the first thing about men", "his sort are the easiest of the lot", these were echoes of Rachel's own secret thoughts. She knew she would never be able to look at a man as—for instance—that busty woman in the Derbyshire inn had looked at Jonathan. Nor would she attract such looks from men as

Jonathan had given the woman. Did that mean there was something wrong with her? But Luke had been attracted. So had Rupert. *Rupert!*

Her heart ached. No more walks along the river with him. Nobody to play tennis with, to fight with and to fall about laughing with. No more sitting together on the top of this hill watching the clouds race across the sky, turning the hillside brown, then moving on over the clustered cottages, the Victorian houses and the church. Watching them now, she noticed how sharp the colours were when the clouds had passed, how gilded the church spire looked and how the river flashed. When the shadow passed over the colliery she was surprised that there was no diminution of noise.

Rupert. Rupert married to Marilyn. She began to weep. Later, as she dried her eyes she told herself it was out of sympathy for him. Because she felt sorry for Rupert. Not herself.

All the same—everybody seemed to be deserting her. Not deliberately, but just taking their happiness where they found it. Not only Rupert—but Mary and David too. From hints they had let drop, it wouldn't be long before David was seeking fresh fields in the North, taking Mary and the twins with him. Amy was becoming more and more involved with her charities. Father was quite happy in Norfolk with his new wife, and when Mummy came home she and Alek wouldn't want her, Rachel, playing gooseberry. There was nobody at all really who was the least bit bothered about her.

Except Jonathan. Again, she went over in her mind the incidents which proved to her that he cared. Brick by brick she built a case for herself. Strengthening her dreams and desires with anything which came to hand; reading all the signs in accordance with her wishes.

Why shouldn't she—? Gradually, the half-formed thought grew and gained strength and conviction. Why shouldn't she go to Italy with Jonathan? True, she would have to take the initiative, and convince him that her age was no obstacle. But what was wrong with that?

And if she couldn't convince him? Well! She thought of Marilyn. What men wanted, she decided, was not a cool and pretty face, interesting conversation and a clever mind but—

She left the thought unfinished and smiled to herself as she walked down the hill. "After all," she said in a near echo of Marilyn. "I'm a woman aren't I?"

12

RACHEL studied herself in the mirror. Apart from the flush in her cheeks she didn't look any different from when she went out. A fact which seemed to surprise her, considering the decision she had come to.

She shifted her glance to Amy's reflection and envied her. Envied her serenity, the control she seemed to have over herself.

"Why are you staring at me like that?" Amy asked without looking up from the book she was reading.

"I was wondering if you'd heard about Jonathan? He's going to live in Italy. Did you know?"

"Yes. He told me some time ago. In confidence. That's why he went there in the spring, to settle the details."

Rachel wore a baffled expression. "Will you miss him? I mean, is he a special friend or anything?"

Amy laughed. "I'm not nursing a secret

passion for him if that's what you mean. I hardly ever see him these days."

Rachel knew her aunt too well to expect her to mention Lena's association with him. As for herself, she couldn't talk about Rupert and Marilyn.

"Amy, may I ask you a personal question?"

"Is the answer important to you, or would you be asking out of curiosity?"

"Terribly important. I want to get things straight in my own mind."

"Ask away then."

Rachel licked her lips and cleared her throat. "Well, you seem so adjusted, as though life had never touched you. I wondered—have you ever been in love? I mean, you are so serene, so self-contained. I'd love to be like you."

"Oh I'm not—" Amy looked thoughtful. "Well, perhaps. The thing to do you know, is take life as it comes. Take each happy moment and enjoy it—"

"And the unhappy ones?"

"They pass."

"So do the happy ones."

"You are rather young for bitterness. What's the trouble? Rupert?"

Rachel didn't answer but she looked so downcast that Amy nodded to herself.

"Surely there's no problem?"

At the gentleness in her voice Rachel's eyes filled with tears. Oh if only she dared confide in Amy. She had the most curious feeling that if she could talk to someone about her obsessive love for Jonathan, the pain caused by its intensity would go away. Like an abscess heals once it has broken. She caught herself up quickly, shocked at the analogy.

Amy was running a finger up and down the spine of her book. "Would it help you to know that after several slight love affairs I experienced a grand passion when I was at an age to know better?"

"What's age got to do with it?"

Amy smiled and turned over a page.

"Could you have married him?"

"If I'd wanted to—"

"But you sacrificed yourself for your father? Is that it?"

Amy burst out laughing. "Not me. I'm the selfish type. That's why I never married. No—if I'd wanted to marry, I would have made my father fit in with my life, not I with his. But I wanted safety."

"I don't understand."

"You wouldn't yet." She thought for a moment. "There's too much responsibility involved in caring for other people. I did not want the responsibility which goes with love."

"Is it a responsibility?"

"I think it is. But it's no good lecturing you about it. It's something you'll recognise for yourself when—if you are in love. The real thing, I mean?"

Rachel ignored the query in her aunt's voice. "Have you ever regretted your decision not to marry—whoever it was?"

"There have been occasions when I've felt sorry for myself but I have the consolation of knowing that had I married him those occasions would have occurred with greater frequency."

"Oh Amy! I never suspected you of being a cynic."

"I prefer to call myself a realist. Look love, have your dreams, enjoy them. Live, love and laugh while you can, but keep your feet on the ground. And if it's Rupert you want, go out and get him. I'm sure he's only passing the time with Marilyn because—"

228

"And how!"

"Pardon?"

"Nothing. Amy, suppose I wanted somebody whom you, and other people thought unsuitable. Would you still tell me to go ahead?"

Amy's face was grave as she watched Rachel's quivering lips. "What you must do is ask yourself if anybody would be hurt by your actions and remember *anybody* means you too."

"Nobody would be hurt."

"In that case," Amy shrugged. Her face was full of dismay. "Are you in love with Luke?"

"As if I would play second fiddle to a motor bike." Rachel laughed and kissed Amy. "Bless you darling. You've helped a lot."

Everything was clear in her mind now. If you wanted something from life, however foolish and unconventional it seemed to others, if it hurt no one, it could not be bad.

There was a glow about Rachel as she walked to the studio the following

229

morning, as though the beautiful weather had permeated her with its radiance.

Borne along in the grip of a strong romantic urge, she could not have stopped now even had she wanted to. She was going along to offer to Jonathan all her love and hero-worship and she did not stop to think that her concept of love might be totally different from his. Not once did she stop to think of the risk she was taking. Not once did she stop to think.

She had rehearsed what she would say until she was word perfect. She had thought of the arguments he would raise and she had her answers ready. There was no doubt in her mind of the outcome because she was thinking positively.

I will. *I will.*

"You look like a buccaneer," she told him. Gently, she touched the bruised cheek. The swellings had gone down and the cuts on his forehead had reached the crusty stage. Rachel's eyes were solemn as she thought how lucky he was not to have been killed too.

"Are you going somewhere special?" he asked. "You look uncommonly smart."

"No," she smiled and looked at the sherry decanter on the marble-topped table. "I'm going home to eat my lonely lunch. Would you care to offer me a glass of sherry?"

Her friendly smile concealed a wildly beating heart. She willed herself to stop trembling, to breathe normally, not to blush.

"What? Oh yes. I beg your pardon." There was a note of respect in his voice she had not heard before.

He poured the sherry and opened a can of beer for himself. "What have you done to yourself? You look different—"

Rachel looked at herself in the long mirror. David had sold her the white suit she was wearing and like all his designs the beauty of it lay in the simplicity and the excellence of the cutting. "Makes you look too old," David had grumbled. "Time I grew up," she had answered. With the suit she was wearing antique earrings and bracelet which she had borrowed from Amy.

Satisfied with what she saw in the mirror, she turned back to Jonathan.

231

"There's a lovely smell. Curry? It's making me feel ravenous."

"Well if Amy has deserted you why not stay and have lunch with me? There's enough for two."

"Thank you. I'd love to. I wanted to talk to you anyway—" She deliberately blocked her way of escape because she felt her courage dwindling. Now she was face to face with him again—looking at the twinkling dark eyes, the silver hair, the vitality of him, her love for him was bright and shining, almost more than she could bear. But her confidence was slipping. In fact, were it not for the sherry—she held out her empty glass in such a way he had no option but to fill it again.

"Is what you have to say to me important or will it keep until we have eaten?"

"It is important but we'll eat first." Apart from the fact that I don't know how to begin, we will have the rest of our lives together if I'm lucky, she thought.

As she drank her second glass of sherry, Jonathan kept shooting robin-bright glances at her.

232

"Why are you trembling?" he asked quietly.

"Somebody walking over my grave," she said. And wished she hadn't. During the silence which followed, she emptied her glass and held it towards him again. "There's a lovely warm glow here." She patted her stomach. "And it's spreading all down my arms and legs. A *beautiful* sensation." She hiccoughed. "Oh lord! Sorry!"

He took the glass from her and laughed. "You've had all the sherry you're going to get here. I'd better see about the food."

He set another place at the table and drew up a chair. "Will madame sit here?"

She moved forward with as much dignity and grace as she could muster and flopped down in the chair.

All through the meal they talked of common-place things. At least, Jonathan did. Rachel heard him through a haze induced by two glasses of sherry on an empty stomach.

The haze had completely disappeared by the time they had reached the coffee stage. So had her confidence. So had her prepared speech. He *would* keep talking!

How could she remember if he wouldn't give her time to think—

She became agitated. Her heart began to thump.

"Amy and I went to an art exhibition last week at the Victoria Gallery." She gabbled at him, trying to bring him back to this room and herself.

"Oh yes? I know." He mentioned the name of the artist. "Did any of his paintings make a lasting impression on you?"

She pretended to give the matter some thought. "I admired his technique," she said at last. "He seems able to construct a dream-world out of nothing." She shot a look at Jonathan. He was listening with absorbed attention, leaning on one elbow towards her across the table.

"Go on—"

"Well—he seems to put in the right touch of colour in just the right place so that it blends easily with all the others. Yet the result is a happy-go-lucky—"

He sat back. "We have one thing in common, you and I."

She looked at him hopefully. "Yes?"

"Yes. We read the same art critic."

Her face flamed. She watched him take

out a cigarette and the long holder. She watched the beautiful hands, the graceful gestures and thought if he hadn't been a successful artist he would probably have made a very good actor. Good to look at. All his movements were studied. He did nothing in a hurry. He blew out a spiral of smoke and smiled at her.

"Don't plagiarise, Rachel. Your own fresh thoughts are worth a bucket-full of clap-trap."

"Sorry."

"You should have known better than to try that on me."

"I've said I'm sorry." All her sophistication seemed to have left her. She thought of Marilyn and wondered how she would have handled the situation. In her imagination she could hear the other girl's raucous laughter at the miserable flop she was making of it. Frozen peas—

"How's that young man of yours?" The friendliness was back in Jonathan's eyes. "What's his name—Rupert?"

Rachel took a deep breath and made herself speak calmly. At last! The opening she wanted.

"Rupert? Oh he's very busy. He has

another girl friend now. Not that I mind. I like him and if he were twenty years older I might have taken him seriously. Even married him if he'd wanted me to. I don't think it's all that important though, do you? Marriage?" When he looked at her without answering she said, "Which do you consider the greater sin, marrying a man you don't love or living with one you do?"

He had been watching her closely. Now he flicked his head sideways and the movement was full of disapproval.

"Don't talk like that. You make yourself sound cheap."

She flinched at his tone but forced a little laugh. "I'm not doing very well today am I? Would you like me to go?"

"Of course not. But you are not doing yourself justice when you talk like that. You know so little of life."

"Perhaps I know more than you think. I may not have had any practical experience but I know what it's all about."

"How lucky you are. I wish I did. Tell me how you know so much?"

"Well I read a lot. Huxley, Lawrence, and all the modern authors who leave nothing to the imagination. I see modern plays and films. Quite frankly, I see nothing to be shocked about."

"But what have such books and films to do with real life, my dear."

"Everything, I would have thought. They are about people, and people are what they are, what they always have been and what they always will be."

"But my dear Rachel, you are not people. You are as unlike the characters in those books as it is possible to be."

Yes? Frozen peas? "How would you know? Or I, for that matter without a practical demonstration?"

Her eyes flickered under his gaze. She swallowed noisily, and her heart beat so fast she thought she would suffocate. But she did not care. She was longing for his love whatever the outcome was, happiness or tragedy.

It was quiet in the studio. A petal fell off one of the roses in the vase he had put on the table. The atmosphere had undergone a subtle change. They sat for half a minute staring at one another. She could not read his expression, but with every fibre of her being she willed him to take what she was offering.

The silence went on for so long a muscle began to twitch under her eye. She put up a hand to cover it.

His voice, when he spoke, was quieter than ever. "Rachel my love, if you've come here for kicks or for someone to initiate you into the seamy side of life, you are wasting your time. You had better run along home.

Run along home! And take your teddy with you? How *dare* he treat her as though she were about ten! She sagged visibly and swallowed the lump that was rising in her throat, and threatening to choke her.

"I haven't come for kicks." She held her breath for half a lifetime, trying to remember her speech. And then the words came out. Not the ones she had rehearsed but an honest outpouring which sounded more like a confession than a declaration.

"I've come because I love you—am in love with you. I want to go with you wherever you go. To look after you. Even if you don't love me. I'm not bothered about marriage. It doesn't mean anything these days. I just want to be with you."

She wasn't looking at him or she would have seen the flicker of a smile which lit his face for a second or two. An indulgent smile which held a hint of satisfaction. The smile of a man pleased the old skills had not left him.

"How old are you Rachel?"

"Nearly seventeen."

He smiled again. This time it was *for* her. He reached across the table and took her hand. He shook each finger gently, separately. This little piggy went to market—? The words flashed across her mind. She snatched her hand away.

"Rachel you are a dear child and I love you very much—"

"I'm not a child," she burst out furiously.

"—But I'm not in love with you or anybody else. My life is exactly what I want it to be. I'm a selfish man. I like to be able to invite pretty women to share a meal with me. I like good conversation when I feel like talking and I like being alone when I don't. I like to stay up and paint all night when the mood is on me and I like to do nothing for days when it isn't. You are very dear to me. All my friends are. But I would not sacrifice my way of life for one of them. Not even you."

She was mute. She sat staring at him. "But I thought—I was sure—" Her face began to work. He got up from the table and so did she. She looked mournfully up at him.

"Doesn't it matter to you that I love you?"

He put his hands on her shoulders and brushed his lips against her hair. "Of course it does. But I don't deserve it. You are a dear little girl and it's time you went home."

For a moment it seemed to her as though she were standing outside of herself watching a TV play. Watching the male lead in a suave, polished performance, with never a wrong word or clumsy gesture.

She twisted away from him and went and stood by the window. The glass was smeary and there was a dead fly in the corner of the sill. All the sounds of summer seemed to drift in through the open transom-light. Children went laughing and shouting along the lane outside. She noticed how clear their voices sounded.

Jonathan came and stood near her. She turned. He was holding out her bag. She pressed herself back against the window ledge and looked up at him. The bony nose, the silver hair curling slightly round his ears, the dark eyes and brows. She touched the bruised cheek. "I wouldn't be a nuisance. I could go to work during the day. You'd be free to do as you liked. And if you wanted to paint through the night —I'm very good at making coffee."

As soon as she said this, she imagined Marilyn's laughter.

Jonathan stood motionless, looking down at her. She knew her face was full of love for him. How could he not be moved?

"Do you know how old I am?"

She shrugged. "Forty-five or six. Does it matter?"

"I am fifty-nine. I shall be sixty in three weeks time."

"You don't look it," she said, genuinely surprised. And her spirits rose. So that *was* it. He was worried about the differences in their ages.

She pulled his head down and kissed

him on the mouth. All her love and knowledge went into the kiss. For a brief moment he held her fiercely then he pushed her away.

Rachel was trembling and ashamed but she was fighting for her love. "You enjoyed that as much as I did."

"Naturally. And now you must go." He put his arm about her and propelled her to the door. "I am deeply moved by your offer. And very grateful. But you must go now."

Again she had the feeling that she was a spectator rather than a participant. And also she felt fear. The love, or whatever it was she had called up was like an evil genie she could no longer control. She was hurt and bewildered and did not know what to do next.

She burst into a fit of childish sobbing. Her face puckered up and she made no attempt to hide it. He moved away and let her cry out her distress.

"I'm so ashamed," she said at last. "I'm going to hate myself every time I think about this afterwards—"

"Never be ashamed of loving anybody Rachel." He put his arm lightly across her shoulders. "Fall in and out of love as often as you wash your hair. But learn to control it. Don't let it control you. Now I'm going to tell you something. I am what I am and I'm too old to change even if I wanted to. But—oh my dear, if I were a *young* man," he lifted her chin and made her look at him. "If only I *were*—"

He put a world of longing into his voice and left the sentence unfinished. The look he gave her would fill her dreams for a long time to come. Suddenly she smiled.

"That's better," he said. "Now I'm going out for a while. Stay as long as you like and if you would care to have one of my paintings, you may help yourself."

He left her and moved over to the alcove where Lena's portrait stood. He looked into the painted eyes for a long time, then he winked, rolled his own eyes upwards and jerked his head back towards Rachel.

He smiled, drew the curtain and went out.

Rachel watched him go. She dried her eyes, mopped her face, powdered her nose and sat quietly taking in the details of the room. She knew she would never see it again.

After a while she moved around the room, touching things; the honky-tonk piano, the book shelves. Moving over to the closet, she opened the door and glanced listlessly at the paintings. Landscapes most of them, with a few abstracts. Nothing appealed to her. Anyway, did she *really* want a reminder of this day? She put the paintings back and was just closing the door when someone spoke behind her. Startling her.

"Can't you see anything you want dear?"

Rachel spun round and found herself gazing through a haze of cigarette smoke at Mrs. Jakes.

"How did you get in? How long have you been here?"

Agitation and guilt made her voice brusque, her manner impolite. Mrs. Jakes raised her eyebrows.

"Long enough." She took the cigarette out of her mouth and blew out a long cloud of smoke without taking her eyes off Rachel's face. "I've got a back door key."

Rachel looked towards the tiny kitchen saw the groceries on the draining board. Remembered David's remark about the thin partition between the kitchen and the main part of the studio. She looked at the open transom light and thought of the children's voices in the lane outside. Mrs. Jakes had no doubt heard something interesting as she walked towards the studio and had crept in quietly. Rachel stood, completely at a loss. Stunned that there should have been a witness to her humiliation. Mrs. Jakes of all people.

But Mrs. Jakes was looking at her kindly. "I could make you a nice cup of tea—"

Rachel shook her head and the tears threatened again. She blew her nose and muttered something about having hayfever.

"You know what's wrong with you, don't you dear? You're like a puppy or a kitten that's been taken from its mammy too soon, or a little bird tipped out of its nest before it's been taught to fly."

Rachel's nerves were raw and tingling. She knew Mrs. Jakes was trying to be kind but she couldn't stand it.

"I know what you're thinking," she snapped. "But I am not the product of an

245

unhappy home. My parents are fabulous. They are tremendous friends still and—"

"All right dear. I'll take your word for it." She drew heavily on her cigarette again and seemed to be considering something. Suddenly she said, "If you can't find a picture you like in there," she jerked her head towards the closet door. "Why don't you look in the divan drawer?"

Rachel stared at her. "Oh, I couldn't do that—"

"Why not? There's nothing in it but paintings." Mrs. Jakes moved over to the divan and lifted the cover. "Look." She pulled out the drawer. It was crammed with unframed pictures mostly on hardboard.

"I'm going home now. Let the snick go on the door when you leave. He never used to bother but he's frightened Mr. Sefton might come in and damage that." She looked towards the alcove. "Lovely picture that." Her voice showed that although she understood the "how" of it, the "why" left her completely baffled. "Going to have a look at them in the drawer?"

Rachel nodded. "I'll have a quick glance." Suddenly she felt sorry for the way she had misjudged Mrs. Jakes. She was quite kind, really. She smiled shyly. "Thank you, Mrs. Jakes," she said.

Mrs. Jakes nodded, blew a cloud of smoke and waddled off.

Rachel watched her walk down the lane and then she knelt by the divan.

Most of the paintings were of local scenes. There was the church, the inn, scenes by the river. Even the colliery winding gear and headstocks had been used and given a stark dignity which, in her present mood, Rachel found appealing.

The next picture was lying face down. She turned it over and found herself gazing into the cool stare of Amy's eyes. It was a head and shoulder study and Rachel sat trying to read something from the expression. Was Jonathan the subject of Amy's "grand passion"? There was no way to tell. She looked at the date. Good heavens! Fifteen years ago! The realisation that she would have been only one year old when this was painted did more to emphasise the generation gap to Rachel than anything else.

Miserably, she reached for the next picture. A full length of Amy in the pose Rachel had seen her in the other day. Book propped up in front of her on the table, head lowered on to hands. Rachel marvelled at the serenity of it. Though she lacked technical knowledge she realised that as in the Sefton portrait, he had not just painted a picture of a woman, but had captured the essence of her. One could tell Amy's character and life-style, just by looking at the portrait.

She searched the drawer quickly, looking for more pictures of Amy, hoping to find one which would tell her what she wanted to know.

The last painting was almost as big as the drawer and was wrapped in a piece of newspaper. The date on the paper and the painting corresponded. Two months ago nearly.

Shame, humiliation and disgust hit her like a physical blow as she looked upon the nude. The white skin of the legs, the pubic hair, the full young breasts, the silky fair hair and blue eyes of Marilyn.

Every brush stroke had been laid on with loving care. The skin had a living, breathing quality. Marilyn's parted lips looked moist, her eyes limpid. It was a portrait of a woman newly awakened. A portrait of fulfilment. Even in her misery, Rachel had to admit to the beauty and artistic talent inherent in it, and two other smaller ones wrapped up with it. Each pose was different but one thing was common to all of them. The sense of involvement, of connivance, of shared knowledge.

She could stand no more. Leaving the paintings on the floor, she ran out of the studio.

Her first impulse was to run home, pack a bag and leave. Instead, she turned the other way to the hill behind the farm. At the top, she flung herself down and hoped to die. Meanwhile she raged. Not against Jonathan but against Mrs. Jakes who had led her to the portraits; against Marilyn, who had succeeded where she, Rachel, had failed.

Humiliation bit deep into her flesh. Rage and jealousy consumed her. (A voice, not acknowledged until later, suggested that she was free. That a heavy burden had lifted but the voice was swamped by her misery.)

After a time the rage subsided and the humiliation turned to self-pity. Rachel wept and when she had finished with her grief she fell into an exhausted sleep. She slept for a long time.

The wind swished through the grass. Down below, the river grew dark, its surface broken and distorted. The head-stocks looked sharp and black against a sky which had turned the colour of a dirty blanket.

Rachel sat up and looked at her watch and disbelieved what she saw. Shivering with cold but disinclined to move, she sat with her arms locked around her knees and looked about her, feeling totally isolated. Disorientated.

What was she doing here? Her memory a blank, she made herself think of all the men down the mine working like moles; girls in offices and shops thinking about their boy friends; road accidents, tangled metal, ambulances carrying away smashed bodies like Lena Sefton's—

Memory returned with a jolt and after

the first wave of nausea she saw herself as she really was with all her motives in perspective. The enormity of what she had done, what she had tried to do, suddenly struck her and she was appalled.

With this new sense of self-awareness came the knowledge that everything was her own fault. Her misery, humiliation, loneliness—all her own fault. Not content with loving someone—if you could call it love—she had wanted to possess him, to be part of his life, his fame. Self-glorification, that's what it was. She had hypnotised herself and battered herself against him. The resulting bruises were the fault of no one but herself.

Self-knowledge gave her strength. She got up and walked slowly down the hill, wondering at the sense of freedom seeping through her. In a strange way, she felt glad for what had happened.

She had been a fool. All right! But everybody makes a mistake at least once in their lives. Hers had cost her Rupert, and her chance of love. It had cost her her self-respect. But there was something she could do. There was the book she was going to write. Now. While her memory was fresh and her emotions raw, she would start her book. She would write until she became famous. What a laugh she would have then at her sixteen-year-old self.

At half past two the following morning Rachel crawled into bed. Her back ached, so did her head. Her eyes were filled with red-hot sand, or so it seemed. The waste bin and the floor around it was littered with torn pages from her exercise books. On the table was one half sheet filled with writing and most of that was crossed through.

No sex-appeal. No literary talent. Nothing. She yawned, noticed the red glow in the sky. "Red sky at night, shepherd's delight," she muttered. And was immediately asleep.

13

BUT the red sky that night was nobody's delight, for the glow came from the fire which gutted the studio and nearly cost Jonathan Blake his life. He was back in hospital after having been found wandering about the meadow, dazed with shock and the pain from the burns he sustained while trying in vain to save the Sefton portrait.

David's workroom was filled with chattering women when Rachel arrived, pale, with dark shadows under her eyes, but quite composed.

David had given up all idea of work and he and Mary were handing cups of coffee around.

Speculation was rife even though it wasn't known for sure if the fire had been started deliberately.

Henry Sefton was the chief suspect, for Henry had disappeared. According to his old housekeeper who had reported his disappearance to the police, he had gone down to the local about nine o'clock the previous evening, something he hadn't done for months. She had gone to bed an hour later and did not know until she went into his room with his morning tea, that he had not been home all night. She had not known about the fire either. Her room was at the back of the farmhouse, she was very deaf and a sound sleeper.

So Henry was the chief suspect. Rachel listened to the women and sent up a little prayer of thankfulness that it was Henry and not herself they were discussing.

"He must have taken a drop too much, hung about the studio till he thought Jonathan was asleep and then tried to get rid of both him and the portrait—"

"Everybody knows Henry hated him—"

"Attempted murder," they said. "Bet he's done away with himself," they said.

And then Rachel heard Marilyn's name mentioned at the far side of the room. Soon, it was being tossed around by them all.

"Everybody knows she was carrying on with him."

Everybody? Everybody except Rachel.

"Always hanging about that meadow she

was, waiting for him to invite her in when the coast was clear."

"So?"

"Well. Suppose that brother of hers got wind of it?"

"Him? He'd be more likely to burgle the place than set fire to it."

"He could have set fire to it to cover his tracks. And what if he found some pictures of Marilyn. Nude?"

Rachel remembered the portraits she had left on the floor. The open door.

"But," said someone, "How can you suspect Henry Sefton and Marilyn's brother and not suspect Marilyn's boy friends. Luke and that red-haired fellow. What's his name? Rupert?"

Rage boiled inside Rachel. She looked round at the women. Kindly folk most of them. Wives and mothers. Dressed in summer frocks and carrying shopping bags. Arms and faces reddened or browned or freckled by the sun. The same expression in all their eyes. Excitement. Somebody had erred. *Somebody* must be made to pay.

But not Rupert. How *dare* they say such things about him! He was the kindest person—he hadn't a mean thought in him He would be the last person in the world to do a vicious thing like that even if he was—if Marilyn was—

Suddenly she forgot the chattering women. Something was happening to her. A warm brightness seemed to be starting deep inside her as she remembered what Marilyn had said. "I missed last month. If it don't come tomorrow I reckon I'm preggy." She was remembering too, the newly awakened look on the portrait of Marilyn and the date of the portrait.

There was a joyous clamour in her head. She was sure, absolutely sure now, that Marilyn had lied about that as she had lied and cheated about other things. It was Jonathan, *Jonathan*, not Rupert who was responsible for Marilyn's pregnancy.

And she marvelled at herself that she could be glad.

Her muscles tightened involuntarily, ready to carry her to Rupert but almost immediately her brain flashed the message. Mrs. Jakes! Her body sagged, as she thought of what Mrs. Jakes would have to say about her, and what it would sound like by the time the gossips had finished with it.

And then Mrs. Jakes sidled into the room. Her first act was to pick up an ash tray and use it and keep on using it until somebody noticed.

Rachel saw David and Mary exchange significant looks, then David crossed the room.

The chattering stopped. David dropped his quiet threat into the silence.

"If I catch you letting so much as a spark or one bit of ash fall on this floor I will cut you into tiny little pieces and feed you to your own hens."

Mrs. Jakes's face quivered. "I know what you must be thinking David. But it wasn't me. Honest. That was no accidental fire. It was started by someone who had a grudge against Mr. Blake."

Her eyes searched the room and settled on Rachel who stared back like a trapped rabbit. She had forced herself to come here this morning knowing what she was letting herself in for. She had looked on it as a form of penance but now a dreadful suspicion was forming. Something so awful she nearly cried aloud.

Mrs. Jakes was still staring at her, her face expressionless. Was she going to tell these women and David that after Rachel had offered herself to Jonathan and he had refused to take her, she had found the pictures of Marilyn and had been so mad with jealousy that *she* had come back later and—?

"That's my opinion," Mrs. Jakes was saying. "Somebody had a grudge against him."

Footsteps on the stairs. The village policeman was young and his face went pink when he found himself confronted by so much femininity but he looked with interest at the half-finished garments hanging on the rails and he grinned at David who handed him a cup of coffee.

"Found Henry yet, Bob?"

"Not yet, but we will. Don't mind me, ladies. This isn't an official visit. But if anybody has any ideas about anything we'd be glad to hear from them."

He sipped his coffee and waited.

The comments were slow at first and directed at him rather than to him. His smile was friendly his eyes alert.

After a while, Mrs. Jakes mentioned

importantly that she cleaned for Mr. Blake and that she'd heard him and Henry Sefton quarrelling—

The policeman nodded. "Were you there yesterday, love? At any time?"

"Yes. Twice. In the afternoon and then again later. I took him some eggs from my fowls but he wasn't in. I put them on the kitchen table and left."

"You have a key?"

Rachel remembered the door she had left open, and held her breath. Mrs. Jakes merely nodded.

"Was anybody else there? Either time—?"

"Only Rachel."

There was a rustle like a soft breeze as they all turned to look at her, remembering who she was. Amy Forester's niece. She spent a lot of time up there—she went on sketching trips with him—they were trying to remember if they'd heard anything else about her. She could see it in their faces.

The silence was almost lethal. Rachel felt as though she were suffocating. Here it comes. The moment of truth. The moment Mrs. Jakes was waiting for.

Over an infinite distance the voice came to her.

"Rachel was there in the afternoon, weren't you dear? In fact she had lunch with him. Mr. Blake thinks the world of her. Treats her like his own daughter. I heard them laughing and talking while I was in the kitchen. When he went out I heard him tell her to choose a picture to remember him by because he's leaving. I showed her where they all were but she didn't want one. Bit old fashioned for you, weren't they dear?" Mrs. Jakes smiled at Rachel. "I put them away and locked up."

"And you didn't see anybody else?"

"No."

"Ah well." The policeman put down his cup, and smiled around the room as he prepared to leave. "I expect we shall find out Mr. Blake was smoking in bed. Fire Officer thinks so anyway. So all we're worried about is finding Mr. Sefton. Sarge seems to thing he might be suffering from loss of memory. Thanks for the coffee David. Keep your eyes and ears open ladies."

He looked mischievously round the

room and then clattered down the stairs.

Rachel stood on the foot-bridge looking at the charred ruins of the studio, wondering how long it would be before the whole village had the same look of desolation. She tried to imagine it as it would be after the bull-dozers and the speculators had done their work. She sighed and was about to move away when Luke came clumping towards her.

He was thinner and paler than before the accident but his bold eyes were full of laughter.

"Luke! How nice to see you. Mind you don't get your crutches stuck in the gaps—"

He grinned and swung himself towards her. "Ay, you can't half nip about on these things when you get used to them." He stood looking down on her. "Go on. Tell me I've spoiled my pretty face. Everybody round here seems to think it's a joke."

"Poor Luke. Never mind, you can always say you got your scars fighting a duel—"

She broke off as the grin on his face was replaced by a scowl.

"I'd like to fight a duel. Right now I would." He sent a brooding look in the direction of the ruined studio. "Fooled me proper, she did. Yet I should've guessed. She never wanted to go anywhere else round here. Always wanted to come down this meadow. Showing off to *him* all the time." He looked at Rachel. "The only one she couldn't get down here was Rupert. God! It made her flamin' mad. Mind you, he never knew what he was missin'."

Rachel felt a flush of love and gratitude for Rupert but she made herself concentrate on Luke and his troubles. Had Marilyn told him herself, she wondered or had he only heard rumours?

"How *is* Marilyn?"

Luke didn't answer. He rested on his crutches and scowled at nothing in particular. Suddenly, without looking at her he said, "I don't suppose you've changed your mind? You know, what we talked about before? Before this?" He patted his plastered leg.

"Oh Luke—"

"You've still got first chance. Mind you,

I'm not waiting for ever. I've got my life to live."

Rachel's laughter bubbled over, glad that the old arrogance was back. "What about that pretty Jamaican nurse?"

"Wow! She's—Aye! You're not jealous are you?" He looked at her hopefully.

"No. I'm not jealous, Luke."

"Pity. That means 'no' then?"

"I'm afraid so. Sorry."

"Oh that's all right." He looked down at the basket of fruit standing at her feet. It was tastefully arranged, with Cellophane and a blue ribbon bow. It looked very expensive. "Are you taking that to the hospital. To *him?*"

Luke seemed unable to mention Jonathan by name. Rachel shook her head. "It's for Mrs. Jakes. She's a great friend of mine and she's not too well. The shock, you know. I think she's very upset and frightened people will blame her for the fire."

Luke had a one-track mind. He was not interested in Mrs. Jakes.

"Oh well, if you won't have me I suppose I'll have to marry Marilyn. Got to have somebody to look after me. Can't

even cut my own toe nails wi' this on."
He tapped the plaster again. There was a
little silence. "Did you know she got
herself in the club?"

"With a little help from someone."

He nodded. "She reckons it's me." And
as Rachel looked at him, remembering the
portraits and thinking her own thoughts,
she was amazed to see a look of pride come
over Luke's face. He smiled, squared his
shoulders. "An' I reckon she could be
right," he said.

David was at his most shrill. "*Would* you
believe it! There they were, the *whole* of
the Nottinghamshire Constabulary out
looking for Henry. And all the time, he
was in your bed. Such goings on!"

Miss Guilford, pink and not at all
unhappy to be the target for a bit of good
humoured leg-pulling, pointed out that she
was a nurse after all. So, when she found
a man obviously unwell, staggering about
outside her cottage late at night, what else
could she do but take him in and put him
to bed? In the spare room, David. In the
spare room.

"And I made him promise afterwards

264

that when the new bungalows are built, Mrs. Jakes and myself will be given priority."

"Good for you, ducky," said David when the laughter had died down.

"And David, I would like to wish you and Mary happiness and success in Newcastle. Don't forget your old friends will you?"

"Bless you. Is it likely?" he said. "Anyway, we shall be back for Rachel's wedding. I'm going to make her the most fabulous gown you ever saw."

Miss Guilford looked at Rachel who was remembering the last time she had been to a party in this room. There were fewer people this time. No Lena Sefton prowling around like a tiger. No Henry drowning his misery as he watched her. No brown-faced stranger with pewter coloured hair and robin-bright eyes—

She herself, felt years older both in age and experience. Perhaps that was why, despite the laughter, the party seemed to her a little on the flat side.

The door leading into the hall opened slowly. Miss Guilford said, "Are you going to be married Rachel?"

Rachel looked at the man who had just come in and her heart overflowed with her love for him.

"Rupert," she murmured. And to Miss Guilford, "I hope so. Oh I *do* hope so."

THE END

GUIDE
TO THE COLOUR CODING
OF
ULVERSCROFT BOOKS

Many of our readers have written to us expressing their appreciation for the way in which our colour coding has assisted them in selecting the Ulverscroft books of their choice.

To remind everyone of our colour coding—this is as follows:

BLACK COVERS
Mysteries

*

BLUE COVERS
Romances

*

RED COVERS
Adventure Suspense and General Fiction

*

ORANGE COVERS
Westerns

*

GREEN COVERS
Non-Fiction

ROMANCE TITLES
in the
Ulverscroft Large Print Series

THE SHADOWS
OF THE CROWN TITLES
in the
Ulverscroft Large Print Series

FICTION TITLES
in the
Ulverscroft Large Print Series

Enquiry	*Dick Francis*
Flying Finish	*Dick Francis*
Forfeit	*Dick Francis*
High Stakes	*Dick Francis*
In The Frame	*Dick Francis*
Knock Down	*Dick Francis*
Risk	*Dick Francis*
Band of Brothers	*Ernest K. Gann*
Twilight For The Gods	*Ernest K. Gann*
Army of Shadows	*John Harris*
The Claws of Mercy	*John Harris*
Getaway	*John Harris*
Winter Quarry	*Paul Henissart*
East of Desolation	*Jack Higgins*
In the Hour Before Midnight	*Jack Higgins*
Night Judgement at Sinos	*Jack Higgins*
Wrath of the Lion	*Jack Higgins*
Air Bridge	*Hammond Innes*
A Cleft of Stars	*Geoffrey Jenkins*
A Grue of Ice	*Geoffrey Jenkins*
Beloved Exiles	*Agnes Newton Keith*
Passport to Peril	*James Leasor*
Goodbye California	*Alistair MacLean*
South By Java Head	*Alistair MacLean*
All Other Perils	*Robert MacLeod*
Dragonship	*Robert MacLeod*
A Killing in Malta.	*Robert MacLeod*
A Property in Cyprus	*Robert MacLeod*

MYSTERY TITLES
in the
Ulverscroft Large Print Series

Murders Anonymous	*Elizabeth Ferrars*
Don't Whistle 'Macbeth'	*David Fletcher*
A Calculated Risk	*Rae Foley*
The Slippery Step	*Rae Foley*
This Woman Wanted	*Rae Foley*
Home to Roost	*Andrew Garve*
The Forgotten Story	*Winston Graham*
Take My Life	*Winston Graham*
At High Risk	*Palma Harcourt*
Dance for Diplomats	*Palma Harcourt*
Count-Down	*Hartley Howard*
The Appleby File	*Michael Innes*
A Connoisseur's Case	*Michael Innes*
Deadline for a Dream	*Bill Knox*
Death Department	*Bill Knox*
Hellspout	*Bill Knox*
The Taste of Proof	*Bill Knox*
The Affacombe Affair	*Elizabeth Lemarchand*
Let or Hindrance	*Elizabeth Lemarchand*
Unhappy Returns	*Elizabeth Lemarchand*
Waxwork	*Peter Lovesey*
Gideon's Drive	*J. J. Marric*
Gideon's Force	*J. J. Marric*
Gideon's Press	*J. J. Marric*
City of Gold and Shadows	*Ellis Peters*
Death to the Landlords!	*Ellis Peters*
Find a Crooked Sixpence	*Estelle Thompson*
A Mischief Past	*Estelle Thompson*

NON-FICTION TITLES
in the
Ulverscroft Large Print Series